DRUID

DEATH WAVE CHRONICLES BOOK 2

ANDRE JONES

ALIEN
PRESS

This is a work of fiction. Names, characters, businesses, places, events, locales
and incidents are either products of the author's imagination or used in a
fictitious manner. Any resemblance to actual persons, living or dead, or actual
events is purely coincidental.

www.andrejonesauthor.site

ISBN: 978-0-6489105-8-9 (paperback)
ISBN: 978-0-6489105-9-6 (ebook)

 A catalogue record for this
book is available from the
National Library of Australia

DEATH WAVE CHRONICLES

To save humanity, civilisation must be destroyed.

Nature is brutally harsh. She plays no favourites, and she rarely gives a second chance. Humanity had its opportunity …

Now it's her turn.

The Death Wave Chronicles is a blend of mythology, 'weird science', fringe science and pseudoscience. Throughout the storyline — more so in some novels than others — I will touch on subjects such as Gaia myth, Earth chakras, the power of crystals, ley lines/earth energy grid, druidism, UFO's, aliens … even Atlantis.

I hope you enjoy the read.

CHAPTER ONE

RHYLLIEN OPENED HER EYES. THIS TIME SHE WAS FAR MORE LUCID during her trance and could easily recall the many visions. Some were reminiscent of her previous interment; other visions were newer — or she had simply forgotten them?

Her recovery this time was swift. As she slid off the crystal bed and started dressing, she replayed the visions in her mind. They were guides to what she had to do and an idea of how to do it. Like it or not — and she didn't — her unique connection to the natural environment made her the ideal candidate for the role of saviour.

"Saviour?" she muttered. "To save the world?" She pulled her boots on. "I just want to be a kid!" she yelled into the emptiness, voice echoing in the dark depths.

At the time of her disappearance thirty-five years before, indigenous tribesmen had stepped in to prevent her death. They'd used blowguns to take care of the strange interlopers who were about to kill the one with the spirit of their Collari, their Incan Queen.

Part of her mind rebelled. *Why didn't they save my father?*

The bed now pulsated the same orange as the diamond she'd placed in its niche. She felt the floor vibrating, not earthquake-like shaking, but a gentle, soothing vibration. Whatever she had done, something had changed.

This region was considered a high energy earth chakra because two prominent ley lines intersected here: the Plumed Serpent and the Rainbow Serpent. These two energy lines in particular crossed six of the seven earth chakras.

From her readings with Nala, this area was believed to be the second, or sacral, chakra, "where primal energy starts to *birth* itself, and that through this chakra the earth overcomes entropy". Another myth stated this was the birthplace of all Inca culture; Inkarri was king, the father and Collari was queen, the mother.

No vision or explanation as to why Giza, another designated chakra region, wasn't on either line, but was still a vital area.

The task given her was straight forward: go to each of these locations and repeat the process she completed here. Failing to complete the task — failure to activate *all* chakras — meant the imbalance would not be overcome. *Everyone* would die.

"Sure, easy." She picked up her pack. "How the hell do I get there? No astral out-of-body-experience travel, I guess?"

The silence didn't answer. Rhyll collected the sun-disc which lay on the side of the bed. "What other doors can you unlock?"

More silence.

She pocketed the disc and took another stroll around the area, marvelling at the workmanship that had gone into the statues, considering these had been here for thousands of years, long before the Incans.

"If only Father could see this." Unbidden tears trailed down her cheeks. "All the years he worked for this very thing, and I'm the one to stick an alien metal disc into a rock wall."

She remembered her old tablet, and pulled it out and videoed a complete circuit, including the pulsating bed, then retraced her steps and took a photo of every statue and inscription she could find.

Further towards the back, she found a clear prism on a

pedestal. It jogged yet another image from her myriad of visions. *And it was mentioned in her dad's notebook.*

She found her torch and shone a beam onto it. The light rays were refracted onto the near wall in a rainbow pattern.

Rhyll took photos of the prism from different angles, then slid the tablet carefully into the pack. Without fully understanding the reason — it was more an instinctive urge — she lifted the prism from the pedestal.

It was heavier than she first thought and she carefully examined it before wrapping it with the clothes in her pack. This one didn't look like it was diamond.

Part of her wanted to stay here and explore everything. After one last look around and making sure she left nothing behind, she strode purposefully up the large stairway leading to a solid wall. Here was another circular depression similar to the one at Hayu Marca. When she inserted the disc, she didn't fade out; the section of the wall became transparent. Beyond was an uneven, rocky path leading down to a dustbowl bathed in bright sunlight.

Stepping through the exit was like entering a wall of clear jelly — she felt a bit of resistance, and it was cool and damp. After emerging from the other side of the wall she checked herself; she was still dry and there was no residue clinging to her clothes.

Rhyll now recognised this area as the Chincana Labyrinth on the northern tip of the Isla del Sol, another ruin left to the elements. Behind her, the rough-hewn wall stood as solid as it had for a thousand years ago.

Now above ground, she could feel a change around her — a renewed vitality flowing across the land. Following the uneven path, she turned to the south at the first opportunity, ducking through a low, stone archway.

Three tourists lay on the ground. From their positioning it was obvious they had collapsed. As she moved closer, she had flashbacks of the mine and São Lucas. The death wave was here, and at every other chakra location!

Sadly, there was no point in caring for the two elderly males and one female. A cell phone lay on the ground by them, reminding her of her commlink. She immediately activated it and called Cataleya.

"Hey, Cat ... Can you hear me?" She waited eagerly, listening to the faint static and hiss. Checking the volume control, she spoke again. *Nothing.*

She reached for the tourists' cell phone, noting the charge and the battery life — and the *no signal* icon. Not that it mattered: she couldn't remember her mother's number or anyone else's. Sliding it into her pocket, she continued walking south.

Like much of the terrain she'd seen, the land was dry and rocky with sparse pockets of vegetation. During her trek she saw other bodies, some of them children.

That was the hardest. Coming across a body was traumatic enough, but a child! Part of her mind wondered why these children didn't survive like those back in São Lucas. The moment her thoughts touched the subject, more of the visions came back to her; these people died prior to her arrival.

It was her presence alone in São Lucas that was instrumental in saving those natives and children! *She* was somehow emitting energy ... or the crystals were; if anyone within her sphere of influence resonated with her — attuned to the earth as she was — they survived the death wave.

After twenty minutes of walking, Rhyll found herself on a low, grassy hill overlooking the beautiful and pristine waters of the lake. The small herd of llamas were a welcome sight. Like before, animals, birds and insects were the only living thing she encountered. In the distance she saw the mainland, closer to the south and dwindling with the distance to the north. Somewhere directly west of her was Hayu Marca and the mysterious entrance.

Below her a trail led to a cove with a wharf and several boats. As she approached, a sleek rental boat with *Copacabana* on its hull caught her eye. With no one alive on the island to return it, she slipped the mooring lines and boarded. The moment she stepped off the land, it was as if a fog lifted from her mind. Suffering a momentary bout of dizziness, she sat down heavily while waiting for the world to stop spinning.

A water bottle rested in a holder on the dashboard, and she realised how thirsty she had become. Even though the water must be over a week old, she didn't hesitate to drink enough to quench her thirst.

It took only a moment to familiarise herself with the controls before starting the boat like she did with the other speedboat. Again, she activated her comm and called Cataleya.

"Hey, Cat ... Can you hear me?" She hoped being on the water and further away from the land would make a difference. After a few seconds, she tried again.

"Rhyllien? Holy shit. Where are you?"

The boat trip to the marina at Copacabana took just over half an hour. As she approached the pier, she saw many people enjoying the sun and fresh air.

She wondered at that. *Why had the death wave not reached here yet? Did water slow it down or stop it?* Nothing from her vision gave her an answer one way or the other.

A wide road hugged the coast, with many cafés and hotels along the beachfront. Mooring the boat along one of the jetties, she strolled down the esplanade to a café that wasn't overcrowded. Rhyll ordered a snack and coffee to await her friends after using the commlink to update her location.

As she sat enjoying the sun and the comforting sound of people laughing, her attention was drawn to the jetty where she'd moored the hire boat. Several people had gathered near it, pointing towards the road and roughly in her direction.

Even short red hair here will stand out. It was only a matter of time before someone from the jetty found her. No doubt they were wondering who brought the hire boat back without checking in at the office.

"Rhyll? We're almost there." She heard on the comm.

5

"Better meet me around the corner on Calle Rigoberto Paredes. See you soon." Rhyllien gulped the last of her coffee and took her snack with her, leaving some loose change on the plate.

It had only been a few hours between her disappearance and catching up with her friends, but it was a joyous occasion just the same. After the many hugs of relief, people passing-by were showing their curiosity.

"I'm glad you all got out okay. Did those men give you any trouble?" Rhyll asked.

"Hardly, but they did provide us with a car." Cataleya laughed.

"Nice of them to have a people-mover, though nine passengers is still a bit of a squeeze."

"I don't think this is what they had in mind. But enough of that; how the hell did you get here?" Dan asked. "You know you disappeared in a flash of light?"

Aware of the interest the group was causing, Rhyll thought it prudent they depart. "Best to explain in the car. My arrival here has caused some attention already." With all the packs secured on the roof racks, they piled into the car. Benigno and Felipe sat in the front seats, with Marco, Dan and Jose sharing the back bench seat and all the girls crammed in the stowage area in the rear.

Rhyll told them about flying to the city under the Isla del Sol, the crystal bed and the wonders of the cavern. She passed her tablet around so they could see the video and pictures for themselves. Then she told them of all the deaths on the island and what she'd put together from her visions.

Rhyll turned to Nala. "It must be this earth chakra we read about. I felt a change as soon as I left the ground. Water has some affect, but not sure if it's good or bad."

"Is it because of the presence of the crystals that no children died around São Lucas, yet they perished on the island?" Dan questioned.

"I can only guess. The news tells us people are dying in all the chakra locations, but these same high energy areas amplify the crystal's power or whatever it is that enables others to survive. I need to get to all these other high energy areas around the world as soon as possible and place each crystal there. This now all fits in with what those visions have been telling me. The longer it takes, the more people will die. It's only when the energy of these crystals is present that those like us survive."

Rhyll looked outside at the passing terrain. They were heading southeast on Ruta Nacional 2 following a ridgeline between two coves. Coming into view was a bridge spanning the Strait of Tiquina. "Have you heard anything from my mother or from Manaus?"

"Nothing further than what we already know," Cataleya said. "We're going to a military base in La Paz. They'll have more information, and we should report in as well. We have about two hours to go before we get there."

"We have new orders." Cataleya returned and sat at the end of the table, showing her colleagues the notification. "Back to Manaus pronto to help there."

They were sitting around a trestle table in the soldier's mess, a large cafeteria on the base a few kilometres from the airport. Over the distant noise of jets and pods they could hear troops marching, or conducting other exercises.

"Anything else?" Rhyll asked eagerly.

"The Major congratulates us on our success so far. He has also managed to get your mother back to São Paulo in a GHO pod."

"How long before you guys have to leave?" Dan asked, screwing his face up at the horrible coffee taste.

"We're on the 2200 hour pod out of here," Cataleya replied.

"Tonight?" Dan's mouth drooped.

"Obviously keen to get their best people back," Ileana said.

"Can we do dinner? Buy you guys a drink for all you did?"

7

"As long as you're buying," Rhyll said to Dan. "I've spent my pocket money."

"I think I can chip-in," Nala said.

"Maybe a couple of drinks at the bar." Cataleya checked her watch. "It's almost 1630 and we've all still got a debrief at 1700."

"Even us?" Dan asked.

Cat nodded. "They'll know as much as the Major did, so no need to keep secrets." She hopped off the table, wrinkling her nose. "Eu cheiro mal. If I smell and look as bad as you guys, I'm hitting the showers and finding a fresh uniform."

Grabbing their packs, they made their way to the ablutions block.

Dan was following the girls when he heard the guys chuckling and joking behind him.

"Good luck in the *banheiro feminino*," Benigno said.

Looking around, Dan realised he'd passed the *banheiro masculino* and sheepishly, he pivoted and followed the guys.

It was a sombre evening at the military bar. Marcos and Jose had been seconded shortly after their debrief to join a flight to Lima. The remaining group of seven gathered in a dimly lit corner, regaling each other with information about their brief but eventful couple of days.

Dan bought a round of drinks for everyone, including a juice for Rhyll.

Before she forgot, Rhyll asked them to put their phone numbers in the cell phone she'd found, explaining to them where she got it. She also asked if Nala remembered her mother's number.

"Easily, chica. I've been using it for the last ten years. I think you should get a new SIM card, though. It could be awkward if a friend of the previous owner calls."

"Wait. Come with me." Cataleya motioned to Rhyll. To one side of the bar area was a SIM and phone vending machine. She selected one and paid for it. "As you know, troops tend to come and go all the time. Sometimes we forget, damage, or lose phones in the field. These are cheap and nasty but come in handy until you can get to a store and purchase a quality phone."

"You're wonderful. Thank you."

"You'll need to charge it before we can put our numbers in, or before you can activate the new SIM." Cataleya swapped the new phone for the old one and dumped it in the recycle bin.

Rhyll ripped the new cell out of its pack, and held onto it as they walked back to join the others. By the time they returned to the table there was enough of a charge for them all to punch in their numbers.

"Holy shit, how the hell did you do that?" Cataleya asked as she entered her number.

"I'm full of energy." Rhyll shrugged. "It's how I started the boats, too."

"A handy trick."

After a few rounds of drinks and vividly recounted adventures, they exited the bar. A service car was already waiting for them. They said their farewells with hugs and promises to keep in touch.

"Speaking of keeping in touch, I better call Mum." Rhyll spent a few minutes on the phone before rejoining Nala and Dan.

"What are our plans?" Nala asked.

"Mum's going to transfer some credits into your account until she can organise one of my own. She's also booking accommodation at the airport hotel under my name."

"Great," Nala said.

"Do we wait for a taxi?" Dan looked at the empty street.

"I can drive." She waved the car keys at him.

"Lucky us." Dan turned to Rhyll. "How's your mother?"

They started walking to the car park, where Cataleya had parked the car.

"She's mending well. Still tender, but in high-spirits otherwise. I told her about the sun-disc working, and the underground city below the lake. I'll need your help in getting the vid and pictures to her. I think my tablet is way out of date for anything other than taking pictures."

"Sure. We can get you a new one, something from this century, perhaps," Dan suggested.

Nala unlocked the Merc. "Where are we off to?"

"Onkel Motel, Aeroporto El Alto," Rhyll said, hopping in the back and letting Dan ride shotgun.

By the time they arrived at the motel, her mother had organised three rooms.

Rhyll said goodnight to the both of them. "It's been a long day. There's a lot for me to take in and digest. See you guys in the morning." She gave them a quick hug. "And hey," she said as she was about to turn away. "Thanks for being here. I know it's not something any of us ever expected." Rhyll left before they could reply.

Later that night before she fell asleep, Imogen called again.

"Hi honey. I hope the rooms are comfortable enough."

"I'm so tired I could sleep on the footpath."

"I won't keep you up, just a couple of things. For the moment I've transferred funds to Nala's account, which should be available by morning. I'll set-up an account in your name, then you can be independent if the need arises. Last thing, you've some very expensive and unique artefacts that won't normally get through customs. As Nala is still an employee of the University, I'm going to get official Customs Clearance waivers signed by the university Chancellor and his brother, who has some influence in government circles. We'll need all the help we can get. They will be in Nala's name so she'll need to carry these items in a secured case and also have the certificate on her at all times. Love you, and I'll talk again in the morning with flight details. Goodnight."

"Goodnight, Mum, love you too."

CHAPTER TWO

THE TRIO HAD TO CHECK OUT OF THE MOTEL BY 10AM. AS IT WAS still several hours until their flight departed, they made their way to the terminal café, sitting near the back out of everyone's way.

"Gives us time to go shopping for a case," Rhyll suggested to Nala.

"I'll stay here and look after our gear," Dan offered. "There's plenty of good Wi-Fi signal, so I'll search what tablets are available."

"Great, thanks."

The two girls headed out the door, leaving Dan with his eyes glued to his tablet and leg entwined in the backpack straps so no one raced off with them.

In less than an hour the girls were back.

"La Paz airport isn't really that large. The shopping is sparse, but we did manage to find this." Rhyll placed the small, black lockable case on the table.

"Looks solid enough. You realise it's a 'Batman' case?" Dan pointed to the distinctive logo. "Kids' luggage doesn't look very official, even in La Paz."

"The other cases were too big for our needs. We've got the

certificates and security clips. Once we cover the logo with an official sticker, who'd know? Easy."

"Did you see an electronics shop?"

"There's one in the International Departures section; probably a better range of luggage too, but we needed this to get through Customs in the first place."

"Cool. So we pack the case with the diamonds, disc and prism, affix stickers and security tags and go?"

"Sure. Any rush?"

"No. Not really, only that I reckon the other side of the security barrier would be safer. Out in the jungle with ancient artefacts and a billion in diamonds is one thing; driving around in a crowded city knowing someone is after us is something else."

"True enough." Nala opened the case while Rhyll opened her pack. "We'll be ready in five minutes."

Once the new case was packed, locked and tagged, they grabbed their gear and walked to the International Terminal security check-in. Dan kept an eye out as they moved through the airport, but there was no need. It was relatively quiet here as the next flight out wasn't for several hours. They dumped their packs on the conveyor belt for scanning.

Nala pulled out her certificate for the officer. He scanned it into the system and awaited the results. In the meantime, Dan went through passport control first, followed by Rhyll. Her biometric passport chip worked fine. She sighed in relief as she stepped up to the next section.

Dan went through the walk-through body scanner without a hitch and waited patiently for his backpack to come through on the conveyor belt.

Rhyll stepped through. The buzzer sounded before the machine flashed on and off then died. One of the officers asked her to step back. He quickly checked the machine and flicked it on and off to reset. Nothing worked. While a technician was called for, he asked her to step through the adjacent machine.

When the same thing happened again, he looked at her suspiciously.

She shrugged.

"Você está carregando alguma coisa de metal?" he asked.

"No, I'm not carrying anything metal." She remained calm because it was the truth. Other than her clothes, everything was in the luggage on the conveyor belt and she had no other possessions.

His wand didn't work either. Irritated, the officer called for a female officer to take her aside for a physical search.

Dan had his pack and was waiting, deciding whether or not to go back to assist. Rhyll saw him. "It's alright. There's nothing to worry about," she called out.

She was taken into a nearby office by the female officer and given a quick and efficient pat down and a perfunctory search. Returning to the Customs area, she was guided to the conveyor belt.

"Ela é clara," the female officer said to her colleague.

Rhyll gathered her belongings and joined Dan. "See? All clear."

The scanners were still out of commission. The officer used another wand to check Nala for metal. Moments later, she too was cleared to join them.

"No problems with the certificates?" Rhyll asked.

"Nada. All good. Your mum can pack some clout when she needs to." Nala collected her backpack and the trio started looking for a place to sit in the terminal.

"Hey, that's great!" Dan pointed at something the girls were oblivious to. "There's an affiliate lounge here from my Qantas Club membership."

Dan was allowed one guest only; he'd need to pay the extra fee for an extra guest. Once Nala took care of that, they went through into relative luxury.

"Much nicer and safer than the terminal area or any old coffee shop; food and drinks on tap, showers through there, and big TVs to watch. You two chill out here, and I'll go and find a tablet for Rhyll."

"You've got the creds?" Rhyll asked.

"Only if you transfer the funds to me."

"Why would I do that?" Nala replied, then laughed at the look he gave. "Joking." She tapped her phone and made the arrangements.

"Thank you," Dan said as he left.

While he was away, they went through their luggage.

Nala pulled out her threadbare jeans. "We really need to get better clothes."

"I guess," Rhyll agreed. Her clothes were in no better condition. "They seemed to last a lot longer in the bush."

"No. You simply didn't need to worry about appearances as much. Sad reality, chica: if you're wearing rags — and dirty ones — people will treat you like a vagabond."

"All pretty pointless—" Rhyll stopped when her phone rang. "It's Mum. I'll put it on speaker." The nearest group were on the other side of the lounge by the TV, so there was no one to overhear the conversation.

"Hey, Imogen. Glad you're recovering," Nala said.

"Hi, Nala. Thanks," Imogen replied. "Still looking after my girl?"

"You bet, though she does quite well by herself."

"So I hear. Now listen, Rhyll. Apparently there's an HSBC branch, of all things, there now. I've set up an account in your full name. Password is your birth year, yacht name, my birth year. Once they verify you are you, they'll punch a cred-chip in your left hand. Nala and Dan will have one, so they can confirm it's okay, but after what you told me about the bio-chip, I doubt this will worry you one bit. Now you can start paying your own way."

"You're wonderful! Thank you."

"A shame I can't be there with you. Anyway," she continued quickly before any tears were shed, "you got the tickets? Sorry about the flights. I know you wanted to get away as soon as you could, but the earliest flight available to any of the areas you listed was London."

"London's fine. We can see about placing two of those crystals in one go. You did good. Mind you ... the business class tickets was a surprise."

"I'd do First Class if I could, but no vacancies. Dan is well?"

"He's fine. Finding me a new tablet."

"You have some good people with you. I'm sure they'll both take care of you."

"I will," Nala confirmed. "And I'll make sure Dan does too."

"Dan does what?" he said as he walked in.

"Is that Daniel?" Imogen asked. "Hello."

"Hey, Mrs. E."

"Good. I'll leave you kids to organise yourselves. Let me know when you get to Heathrow. And I don't care what time."

"Love you Mum. Bye."

"What's up?" Dan sat down with them, laying a box on the table.

"Mum's organised a bank account for me. I need to get the cred-chip inserted."

"Great, and here's your new tablet. If you want, I'll set up a cloud account ... Pretty sure your e-address will be void."

"You mean for mail? Never had one. I was moving around so much in jungles, why would I need it? The people I met didn't have one either."

"Leave it to me. Go and get your cred-chip and I'll see you when you get back." Dan had been unpacking the tablet, and now plugged in the charger.

The fifteen-hour flight to Heathrow was uneventful, though very comfortable.

Nala and Rhyll were situated in the two central cubicles, with Dan adjacent across the aisle. As Rhyll had never been in Business Class — her one and only flight was decades ago — she was both appalled and amazed at the comfort and facilities available. Her seat folded down to form a bed with privacy screens and a small monitor for entertainment.

"How does all this fit with your environmental values?" Dan leant across after the breakfast trays were taken away.

"Honestly, it doesn't in any way. Don't get me wrong, part of me likes it because of the comfort and ease, but it isn't sustainable, even with trying to be carbon-neutral—"

A chime sounded for an announcement by the pilot. "Ladies and gentlemen, tower control at Heathrow warns us the field is shrouded in fog. With regret we'll divert to Gatwick Airport. Upon landing, please head to the help desk to organise transfers. On behalf of British Airways, we apologise for any inconvenience."

"Is that bad?" Dan asked. Several passengers were heard swearing and complaining.

"Not for us. It's not like we've got anyone waiting. A bit longer for you to drive, that's all."

"Me?" Dan looked surprised.

"I've never driven on the wrong side of the road before," Nala said.

"You kidding? Brazilians always drive on the wrong side of the road."

"You know what I mean," Nala responded.

"If it's like São Lucas, there'll be roadblocks. Did you consider that?" Dan wondered.

"I'm hoping something will turn up. The longer it takes, the more people will die. What was the latest on the news?" Rhyll asked.

"Apparently all the other areas are moving much slower than São Lucas or Manaus, but even so, it's been eleven, maybe twelve, days I think."

"Let's see where the roadblocks are first. Maybe we can sneak through on foot." Rhyll hoped.

"I think we're being followed." Dan checked the rear-view mirror again. They had grabbed a hire car and left Gatwick as soon as they could.

Traffic heading west had eventually dwindled, except that one car behind them. The traffic going east had been non-stop: cars, caravans, coaches and lorries a constant stream of anything on wheels jamming all lanes; motorcycles cruised wherever they could, between the lines of cars, up the emergency lanes and nature strips. It was a tragic accident waiting to happen.

The radio news had been blaring out a warning for everyone in Wiltshire and Somerset to vacate immediately. Traffic was prohibited going into the affected area, with many drones and pods crisscrossing the night sky.

"Followed? Why do you think that?" Nala had been dozing on and off in the back, feeling the effects of jet lag.

"Because I've made several unnecessary turns, and the same car is still behind us; a dark Beamer." He drove on for a few minutes. "I'm going to pull over at this rest stop and see what they do."

"You're sure it's the same car? With this mist, it could be someone else. Maybe Benigno's paranoia has rubbed off on you?"

"Maybe. I'll know after this experiment."

Rhyll had been reading her tablet after uploading all the files from her old tablet to her account. While she was in the lounge, she'd used their facilities to scan her father's notes and give her mother access. Now she could review everything, including the details of the underground city.

"He might have a point. The news says they're evacuating everything west of Amesbury and telling everyone to go as far as they can north or east."

Dan pulled over to the parking area. "Anyone need to use the loo?"

"Now that you mention it ..." Nala sat up and stretched.

"I may as well go, too." Rhyll popped her tablet on the

dashboard, climbed out of the car and joined Nala, traipsing off through the mist to the small roadside café.

Dan watched in the mirror. The car he'd thought was following kept going. He watched until it disappeared over the rise, taillights blurring in the fog.

"Yep. Paranoid." Shrugging, he jogged inside. Staring into the constant stream of headlights had given him a headache, so he ordered a coffee and looked for some medication.

In a few minutes the trio were back on the road again. After another hour of driving in the mist, the eastbound traffic had reduced to a trickle. West of Andover they saw the red and blue flashing lights of emergency vehicles ahead.

"Looks like we found the roadblock." Dan continued, slowing down, expecting the police or the local corporate goon squad to hail them. Having just passed the small village of Thruxton, this section of the motorway had no turnoffs, and making a U-turn now would look suspicious. Two intermittent red lights high in the sky to their right indicated towers.

"I think there's an airfield over there." Nala pointed out, following his glance.

"And that's not a roadblock ahead. Looks more like a truck collision," Dan said as they drove closer to see details through the haze. "Are those placards?"

"Why are they protesting a traffic accident?" Rhyll asked.

Nala opened her fogged window to see clearly, the frigid night air chilling her cheeks and waking her up more. "I think it's a circus. I can see a giraffe on a truck further back."

"It's a crime to have a giraffe out here!" Rhyll protested. "In fact, it's a crime to have most of these animals in England."

"I reckon that's what the placards are for." Dan slowed and wound down his window. "Can you hear that?"

"Stop the car." Rhyll hopped out the moment the wheels stopped rolling and listened; concentrating. "There's an injured animal. He's in pain." She started walking across the empty road, as there were no other vehicles travelling west.

"Wait!" Dan called.

"I can help here," Rhyll continued stubbornly.

"She probably can, too!" Nala climbed out to follow.

Shaking his head, Dan grabbed the keys, locked the car and hurried after them.

Now out of the vehicle with the motor off, many more animal noises could be heard: monkeys, bird-squawking, and various growls.

It was a traffic accident. A convoy of lorries had pulled over, the second and third vehicles at odd angles, and four other lorries behind. There was also a car now visible in a ditch in front of the convoy. It looked like the first truck slammed on the brakes and jackknifed. The next lorry had stopped in time, but the third had run into the back of the second.

Behind the convoy several cars had stopped, and pockets of people were scattered here and there towards the rear having an argument. A number of uniformed people were trying to sort things out.

"What's happening?" Rhyll asked one of the placard wavers. The sign said *Free the animels!*

The tall, thin girl turned to Rhyll, looking her up and down, taking in her new clothes. "Come ta gawk at the pretty animals 'ave we? Piss orf."

"I came to help."

The girl laughed. "As if. Yer credits can't 'elp 'ere. Hey, Simone. Check 'er out. This little ginger says she can 'elp."

"I can. There's an injured lion. He's in pain."

"No shit, Sherlock," Simone scoffed.

Rhyll walked past, deciding to ignore them both.

"Oi! Get back, miss. You protesters have done enough." It was a burly man in overalls with *Long's Animal Park* printed on the front.

There was a TV crew with him asking questions and drones buzzed overhead. They now turned their attention to her.

"I'm a vet assistant," Rhyll lied. "Do I look like a protester to you?" If the girls thought she wasn't a protestor, she could use it to her advantage.

"Nah. But it's dangerous, so get back. There are wild animals on the loose." He briefly explained about the accident, and how the stupid protesters had unlocked some cages.

"Isn't there a vet travelling with them?"

"Still over an hour away, back in Chessington."

"But that lion's in great pain," Rhyll protested, feeling its discomfort.

"Well, I ain't going in there. It'll have to wait." He turned back to the camera.

Still new at stretching out her mind, Rhyll perceived the other animals nearby. Some were still in their cages, some wandered through the trees; there was a lioness staying close to her mate, watching them warily, a couple of camels in the field behind the hedgerow ... and a rhino at the rear, slow to realising its back door was open.

Nala and Dan caught up. Rhyll relayed the information. "Can you distract him?" She pointed to the burly man. "I need to get in there."

"*In* there? With that lion? Are you kidding?" Dan stared at her as if she were mad.

"I gave a wild jaguar a rub-down," Rhyll reminded him. "I'll be okay."

"Yeah ... but ..."

"Tell him there's a lioness over there in the trees," she lied.

"He'll never believe me."

"He will. Tell him her left ear is missing the tip." She gave him a little shove of encouragement. "Go on."

"I'll stay here just in case," Nala said.

"In case of what?" Dan muttered, looking over his shoulder as he walked away. He got the man's attention, describing the lioness as per Rhyll's details.

Summoning two of his lackeys with tranquiliser rifles in hand, the burly man moved off. The cameraman turned and kept recording. Further down the road were other groups of people; protesters, drivers and police.

"I'll let you know if they come back," Nala offered.

Rhyllien nodded and quietly went to the far side of the truck, away from prying eyes.

"What's the ginger doin'?" The lanky girl came over to Nala.

"Something more useful than standing around squeezing pimples and waving bits of cardboard." The irony of her words weren't lost on Nala, considering what she'd been doing the last fifteen years.

At Rhyll's approach, the lion snarled loudly. She sensed its injured leg and back, deducing that when the truck stopped quickly, the lion fell, twisting its leg and spine. It was lying there, front leg sticking through the bars at an unnatural angle.

"Easy, fella," she said in a soothing tone, concentrating on his pain.

His growling softened, sensing a kindred spirit.

Slowly, in an unthreatening manner, she reached out to him through the bars, not only with the hand but her mind. Gently, she then ran her hand up the leg to the injured area. The leg was twisted at the shoulder; dislocated. Not severely, but enough. She knew it as well as she knew about Ileana's fractured elbow back in Brazil.

Rhyll spent several minutes calming him, almost sending him to sleep. She heard Dan and Nala wander closer. "Dan," she whispered. "I'll need your help."

"Me?" He gulped. He saw Rhyll nod. He licked his lips nervously and took a pace closer.

"Closer. All the way."

"I'd rather not."

"All you need to do is hold his paw."

"Hold ... his ... paw? You mean the paw that's larger than my face? The paw with razor sharp claws that could shred me to pieces?"

"Good, you can see it. Don't be a sissy. He'll thank you for it."

"Chewing my arm off is not the thanks I want."

"Get over here." She raised her voice and the lion softly

grumbled in his stupor. "He's basically asleep. Once you have a firm hold, I'll tell you when and how to give it a hard pull."

Dan's face paled.

"Want me to do it?" Nala offered.

"No, no. I got this." He still hesitated.

"Sometime soon. I can't keep this up all night," Rhyll encouraged.

Dan's hands shook as he tentatively grabbed the lion's leg.

"You need to relax and trust me. Slowly tighten your grip. He's unconscious now." Rhyll had one hand on the lion's shoulder, and the other hand on top of his head. She sensed Dan's handhold. "Move them around clockwise. There. Tighter. Both hands. Step slightly to your left. You want to pull in a straight line to realign."

"I'd rather not pull at all," Dan muttered but complied, not taking his eyes off the lion's mouth, expecting to see the huge teeth any second.

"When I nod — look at me! When I nod, give it a hard pull straight back. Okay?"

"Hard straight back pull. Got it." He licked his lips again.

"Three, two, one." She nodded.

Dan let out the breath he'd been holding and pulled as hard as he dared.

The lion roared, eyes flaring, large teeth now clearly visible.

Dan let go, losing his footing and falling against the hedge.

Rhyll stepped back, continuing to talk softly to the lion. "Easy. Easy, boy."

"What the hell? What are you three doing?" A police officer came around the corner, the two protesting girls close behind him.

The lanky girl pointed. "Ginger there's tormentin' that lion. We told 'er not to."

"You stupid lying *puta!*" Nala vented at the girl.

"You, miss. Get back here," the cop called out to Rhyll.

Rhyll ignored him, knowing he wasn't about to get any closer himself. She kept concentrating on the lion until it settled again, noting the pain was much less.

The lion withdrew his leg and stalked around the cage, panting, a limp still evident. At the back of the truck the gate was ajar. He hopped down to the road, still favouring his injured shoulder and sauntered towards Rhyll.

She kept her ground, sensing no threat, but the cop and the two girls moved back nervously.

The lion reached Rhyll and nuzzled against her, almost pushing her over. His massive head lolled lazily to the side, looking at Dan who was nervously getting up off the ground.

Rhyll reached down and gave the mane a big rub. "Good boy." She turned to the others. Nala remained where she was, but everyone else backed away in shock. "He just had a dislocated shoulder. He's better now."

The cop stared. The two girls fled, dropping their placards.

Hearing the noise and sensing a story, the camera crew turned up quickly and started recording. The lion growled at them, but enjoyed the rub Rhyll was giving it.

"Dan?" Rhyll coaxed him over.

Dan nervously stepped closer, sharing a quick rub with it, but moved back. "Your turn," he said to Nala.

Nala, confident after her meeting with the jaguar, slowly stepped up and stroked the lion's flank.

There was a roar behind the hedge.

The TV reporter swore and flinched.

The lion replied with a roar of its own, turned and bounded into the woods, disappearing in seconds.

"Is there a third lion?" Dan asked looking nervously where the first had disappeared.

"Nope."

"Then why did you tell me there was a lioness over in those trees?" Dan pointed across the road.

"Because I wanted that man away from here so I could work. I wasn't going to tell him where the lioness really was."

Now the animal was gone, the reporter walked up to her. "Evening, miss. Brody Thurston, UKTV. How did you do that?" He followed this with many questions. She tried to answer as best she could. In the meantime, more people gathered around to listen.

Dan moved back next to Nala. He turned, hearing smashing glass. "Shit. Those guys are breaking into our car!" He began running across the road towards their hire car. A dark BMW was parked behind it, doors open and motor still running.

Nala looked. "Rhyll. They've got the case!" she yelled.

Looking through the bars of the cage to the far side of the motorway, Rhyll saw two guys run back to their BMW. One held a familiar black case. The driver revved the car for a quick getaway. The tyres spun on the damp bitumen. The Beamer slowly moved, sliding sideways. Easing off the accelerator, the driver allowed the tyres to get more traction and it jolted forward.

Halfway across the nature strip, Dan angled in an attempt to intercept, though what he was going to do against a speeding car was anyone's guess.

The cameraman had now turned to record the getaway car.

Rhyll thought hard. They had the diamonds and artefacts with them! In her mind's eye, she sensed the rhino now free at the back of the line of trucks.

Stop them! she yelled in her head as she ran down the side of the trucks. She repeated the request. *You will all be free from the torment of mankind soon!*

The female rhino, slow at first, pawed the ground and started trotting, sensing the urgency of the strange call in her head. She heard something noisy moving like it was on the chase. Only enemies chased.

Gaining speed after a few long strides she turned, dropping her head as she rammed into the car's side. The car swerved to the side of the road, hit the uneven gravel surface, skewed sideways then flipped over onto its roof, sliding into the ditch as it slowly spun.

Dan, breathing heavily, was first to arrive near the crash site.

He stopped a few paces back while the rhino head-butted the car's front panel repeatedly, guessing the sound of the roaring engine irritated the animal.

Easy, girl. Rhyll ran up, hardly out of breath. *Good girl. Good girl,* she repeated in her mind, sending soothing thoughts. "Dan. You should turn the motor off now."

Dan hesitated for the briefest moment before moving to the driver's door. He dropped to his knees in the long, damp grass, reached in awkwardly for the button and switched it off. He saw one of the occupants lying on his face on the inside of the roof, which was now the floor, his head bent back at an odd angle.

Next to him was their black case.

Dan pulled it out. Through the far window he saw people running towards them. Without looking, he awkwardly flung the case underarm behind him, hoping the bulk of the car covered his actions. It landed out of sight in the field behind.

"It could be difficult explaining the case. We can grab it once they go," he said softly to her.

Rhyll gave the rhino a hard scratch on the neck. "Off you go." She then gave it a smack on the rump.

Without any indication of feeling the slap on her thick hide, the huge animal pushed through the hedge effortlessly and disappeared into the foggy night.

The driver groaned. The second passenger remained unconscious and silent.

Several other police officers, two males and a female who had been talking to bystanders of the initial truck accident, raced over to assist.

"You better call an ambulance," Dan called out to a cop. Trailing the cops, the cameraman and reporter were also jogging up. "This is going to be a long night." He looked to Rhyll, but she was no longer there.

CHAPTER THREE

RHYLL PUSHED THROUGH THE GAP IN THE HEDGE ON THE HEELS OF the rhino. Now she was out of sight, looking at a dark, open field. Oblivious to the goings-on by the road, the rhino nosed through the long grass.

She heard Dan saying it was going to be a long night, and silently agreed. She had to leave so abruptly because there'd be too many awkward questions. Delays meant potential deaths.

Stonehenge—where she was to place the next crystal—was still twenty kilometres away. And judging by the latest news, she'd still need to avoid the roadblocks somehow. Best to get away before any more delays. She'd speak with Dan and Nala on the phone later.

Sensing their location, Rhyll quickly collected the case containing the crystals and artefacts from the long grass and moved off into the darkness towards the camels grazing nearby. She approached cautiously. Like she did with the lion, she made no threatening motion, sending calming thoughts. It was curious: none of the animals were perturbed with the other predator animals currently roaming the countryside, and she wondered if that was her presence, something underlying the energy the earth was emanating, or something else entirely.

She realised now that she was closer, these camels were the two-humped variety—*Camelius bactrianus*, she remembered. Getting to ride one proved easier than she anticipated. As she considered the problem of how to mount, one of the pair dropped down to its knees.

Rhyll hadn't requested or instructed this action, but she quickly realised these animals were probably accustomed to giving rides to children. "And no doubt that's why they're calmer than expected."

It was the male that had allowed her to ride, and with a bit of an effort because of his size, she pulled herself up and straddled the dip between the humps. They were firm, indicating he had been well looked after. When he rose, it was so unexpected that she nearly suffered whiplash. He started walking west. His mate followed.

It took a while to get used to the rhythm of his gait, but eventually she learnt to sway with it. The distance covered with each stride was impressive. Other than the general direction, no guidance was required, giving her time to message her friends. With the truck accident now out of sight, she felt guilty about leaving them behind to answer the awkward questions.

She sent a brief text.

"Heading to closest place. I have everything needed. Will call later." She didn't think it too cryptic, but also didn't want to be too obvious in case others saw it.

"Now who's being paranoid?" she muttered.

Her phone pinged. *"Stay off the roads. DIC is the local corporation. Watch out."*

To the south she saw the flashing lights of the roadblocks, and the nav-lights of hoverpods in the distance.

"DIC?" she muttered to herself. "Lucky for me they're monitoring roads and not fields."

Even though it was dark and foggy, she decided to move slightly further north so they weren't as visible from the main road. The terrain here was agricultural: ploughed fields and hedges with narrow lanes and gates. The rooftops of a small hamlet appeared, the houses mostly dark with only a couple of windows dimly-lit. "Shipton Bellinger," she surmised from her recollections of the map. She hoped the occupants had all managed to get away, but didn't consider checking for herself, having no desire to see more bodies. *And there's nothing I can do for them.*

From the faint buzzing and tiny blinking lights, it sounded like several drones were now also scouring the area. There was no beam of a searchlight.

"Maybe they're using thermal imaging," she guessed. Unphased by the noise, the camels plodded on.

As they neared a fence, she heard a car coming along the lane. She coaxed the camel to stand still behind the hedge. The telltale whir of the tyres reminded her of the large tread of a four-wheel drive. Sure enough, a military vehicle drove past with a spotlight sweeping the fields. It flashed by her, and as the beam flitted through the foliage it briefly illuminated the bulk of the camel. The car continued without slowing, so the occupants plainly hadn't spotted them. Waiting for the sound to dwindle to almost nothing, she moved onto the road, following it until a gate presented itself. Just to the north of the houses she continued through the fields.

Halfway across, the buzz of another drone reached her ears. She ducked low as it flew over and around them. She held her breath, waiting, hoping her heat signature would be mixed with that of the camel's.

The drone moved on after completing a couple of circuits.

It took twenty minutes of negotiating low fences and small creeks before another road appeared heading roughly in the direction she was travelling. It was faster and easier for the camels, so she decided to follow it.

Soon they entered another village, this one larger, with the name on a sign *Bulford Camp*. She thought it an unusual name and as she entered further, she recognised the style of houses and high fences as some sort of military base. Marlborough Road angled south; Stonehenge was close to the main road, and she sensed a faint disturbance in that direction. No bodies were visible, and if it was an army barracks they'd have evacuated already. She considered briefly the useful things she might find in an abandoned military base, but her gut feelings around weapons were always the same: discomfort.

The town dwindled behind, and an orange glow in the fog at an intersection indicated the main road was about a kilometre ahead. On arrival, she discovered the main road was abandoned, as expected. Unlike the roads in Brazil, no derelict cars with deceased drivers or passengers were found.

With the drones and hoverpods way back checking the boundaries, Rhyll directed the camels along the A303 west, passing north of Amesbury. The effects of Stonehenge in the distance were stronger. In the darkness, a large manor house loomed on her right. A sign with an *historic tourist walk* icon stated *King Barrow Ridge.*

She rode on; her next destination was ahead, with nothing stopping her.

Other than the experience with the thieves, and overlooking the long travel, it was a relief to be here now, considering the stress and threat of violence of the previous chakra point.

From her research, this location was the *heart* chakra. As she moved closer to Stonehenge her senses wanted to move her more to the left, though the signage ahead clearly indicated Stonehenge was ahead and to the right. To be sure, she continued towards the large circle of ancient standing stones to see what happened.

There was a disused track veering off to the right, with a large locked gate leading directly to the site. Rhyll paused to consider the options of continuing along the road, as opposed to dismounting, releasing the camels and taking the shortcut on foot.

After a brief contemplation, she decided the camel — and her own rump — could do with a reprieve. Before the camel could drop to its knees, she swivelled, throwing her leg over the front hump with difficulty, and slipped off to the ground. Luckily she landed on the grassy verge, for her legs were numb after dangling for several hours. She collapsed, lying in the damp grass and laughing at her silliness.

The camels regarded her, blinking several times before they both swung their heads to the east. After a pause, they started ambling away along the road, gradually building into a ground-devouring trot.

The soft buzz of a drone reached Rhyll's ears as it descended from high altitude.

She lay in damp grass on the northside of the road with little cover in any direction. Grabbing the case, she tried to stand, but her legs refused to work correctly. She stumbled to the dirt and gravel, grazing her knees and palms painfully, the case sliding across the damp road surface.

"Ow and shit!" she swore, blowing on her skinned palms. She lay there, in the hope the drone was concentrating on the moving camels and would overlook her.

No such luck this time. The heat-signature of her sprawled body no doubt contrasted greatly with the ambient temperature of the much cooler ground. The drone hovered, circling slowly, centring around her.

"And no doubt the troops will be on their way soon enough!" Reluctant to stumble onto the hard road or gravel again, Rhyll sat there until the blood circulation, aided by rapid massaging, brought some feeling back to her legs. She kept her eyes to the east along the A303.

Across the road to the south, the nearest cover of any description was a large copse around two hundred metres distant. She wasn't a sprinter, and considering the long grass and darkness, she'd not be breaking any records. "Probably breaking just my leg or an arm."

Behind her, Stonehenge was open ground for about five hundred metres; the manor house just as far back to the east. When she finally felt ready, she carefully stood up. The sensation of knowing where to go was as strong here and now as it was back on the shores of Lake Titicaca.

Strangely, that direction was south — away from Stonehenge — but it was still close. Very close. Picking up the case, she ambled across the A303 and climbed the old wooden fence into the field beyond. The drone followed, and now she heard the whirring of tyres. From the number of headlights, she estimated three vehicles coming for her, beams of their spotlights sweeping across the open fields.

The large copse of trees became clearer and as she approached, the sensations became stronger. She climbed another fence and covered the distance as quickly as she could.

Too late! A beam of light stabbed her in the darkness before she disappeared in the foliage. She heard splintering wood behind her; possibly the cars crashing through a fence or farm gate.

The sound of tyres on gravel grew louder and there were intermittent headlights through the dense bush.

Within the gloom underneath the canopy of the large trees, she felt an ancient presence. Rhyll couldn't explain it, but was not concerned, sensing no threat. The ground rose, too low to be a hill though she could definitely feel she was moving higher with each step. She recalled there were many burial mounds in the surrounding area — but those were all in fields and clearly visible. "Why was this different? Assuming it was, in fact, a barrow ..."

She started looking for a place to hide. The foliage was thick, but she was sure the army would find her soon enough with thermal imaging. "Why bother?" she groaned. *Because you have a billion credits in diamonds and the fate of the world in your hands!* was her immediate mental rebuke.

The cars pulled up. She could barely see the headlights, it being so dense in here.

If this was a barrow, it was enshrouded by massive boles of oak and elm. Many of these trees must be hundreds of years old — certainly nowhere near the timeframe of even the Incans, let alone the many cultures that dated back thousands of years before them, but much older than the lifespan of a several human generations.

Muffled voices could now be heard. Mostly men, but she did hear a couple of female voices calling for her.

"Come out," she heard from the loudspeakers, and, "It's not safe here!". Then she heard the dogs baying, and in minutes their snorting and huffing as they picked up her scent and pushed their way towards her.

Above, she heard movement; the fluttering of wings, leaves rustling as small nocturnal creatures moved around on their nightly endeavours, foraging for food or materials for their homes before the cold of winter set in.

Rhyll worked her way into the depths of the thick undergrowth. Feeling the ground rise, she came face to snout with a badger. Its whiskers quivered as it sniffed her. She reached out and scratched it behind the ears, after which it calmly moved on. As did Rhyll.

At the top of the rise was an ancient oak with convoluted roots, some of its branches broken and decaying on the forest floor. The tree wasn't imposing in height, but the girth of the trunk was substantial. It was long dead, the indications of a lightning strike evident. The feeling led her to a hollow between the shoulder of two roots, hidden within the darkness and undergrowth.

Two bloodhounds nosed their way through the thick foliage and snuffled to her location. She turned and put her palms out, concentrating. They both stopped their noises, sniffed her skinned palms and let her pat them.

Roughing up their coats, Rhyll knelt between them. "Good boys," she whispered her praise. "Now, off you go." She directed a thought, and the hounds began their braying and continued their push through the foliage.

Torchlight still played over the area, but not near her.

Rhyll had no doubt the soldiers had seen her enter, and while they relied heavily on the hounds, if need be they'd continue searching until the whole copse had been thoroughly covered.

She could still hear drones overhead but the canopy was too thick for them to access.

Focusing on the problem at hand, Rhyll turned and pushed the case in front of her to explore the hollow in the tree-trunk. She crawled inside, relishing the cool freshness of the rich soil and earthy scent. It felt so good! The interior of the trunk was dark and she sensed more than saw how the hollow descended deeper within the ground.

She twisted around in the tight space so she was feet-first and used the roots and rough sides to climb down, eventually finding herself in a vaulted enclosure. It was slumped in some areas, looking like the weight of the tree had pushed it in.

If she was her father, the whole area would be cordoned off, sectioned, and painstakingly searched grain of dirt by grain of dirt; photos, notes, voice recordings ...

Rhyll wished she had her tablet to take photos. The crypt in the centre, cracked and partially open, showed the skeletal remains of a corpse that rodents and bugs that had feasted on, perhaps centuries before. There were also threads of some garment draped across the thorax.

The air here was damp and malodorous, but she persevered. She had to. Outside was too dangerous for the time being, and she hoped they didn't find the entrance; there was no escape from here.

"I've smelt worse." The sound of her voice was flat and softened within the tomb. There was definitely no large crystal bed here. She sat to rest, leaning against the side of the crypt. The pain in her hands impinged on her thoughts.

The healing technique was coming to her quicker each time she used it. Before long, her palms were clear of the scratches; even the embedded grains of grit had been removed.

She rested for a time, absorbing the vibe and energy around her, noting this time she wasn't overcome with weariness, before extracting the green diamond from the case. Like the others, it still glowed and gave a faint vibration; the sun-disc remained as normal.

The prism was still somewhat of a mystery. Her father's notebook contained few mentions of it, and what there was had been water-damaged. The little that she could decipher mentioned something about seven rays of light, and it was written beside a sketch of what she'd thought was a triangle, but now grasped was a prism. On the reverse side of the damaged page were various references to Atlantis and orichalcum.

If it wasn't in her father's notes, there was no way she'd believe anything about the Atlantis myth, but seeing it in his handwriting — even with the smudges — the meaning was unambiguous. According to his findings, Atlantis had been real, and it wasn't based on the writings of any ancient Greek philosophers, but on the clues he had found.

A trickle of dirt down the back of her head broke into her thoughts.

No vision or memory of what to do came to mind. Closing her eyes and concentrating, she held the diamond as if some divine answer would present itself, just the normal tingling sense of calm and warmth.

Nothing.

"Do I just dump you in the dirt?" Using its dull glow, Rhyll held it while she crept around, stooped as it was too low to stand upright. Her boots found several items on the ground covered by centuries of dirt where it sifted through the walls and sagging ceiling.

There was a cracked ceramic urn with a faded Celtic design, various figurines of animals both in wood and ceramic, and a scabbard, now in tatters, enveloping a surprisingly not-too-rusty sword. She decided it practical to leave everything in place and if there was an opportunity to return, then do what her father would have done.

"This might even encourage Mum to revisit the UK." She popped the diamond into her pocket.

With the aid of her phone's torch, the lid of the sarcophagus was next to be examined. Her eyes had been so used to the dim glow of the diamond she had to blink several times against the brightness. She could trace the outline of an engraving. It was a woman, in armour, and possibly carrying a sceptre, but a crack across the stone made it difficult to be sure. A female warrior, perhaps?

At first she thought the figure wore a crown. The engraving had deteriorated over the ages, but it was definitely a head covering of some sort, perhaps a symbol of rank or stature. Rhyll shifted around and looked closer, moving her fingertips lightly over the area. If she had to guess, above the headdress was an engraving vaguely resembling Yggdrasil, the tree of life.

Perhaps she was a high-level druid. She wracked her brain trying to think of any druidic references; the only female druid she could think of was ... *Queen Boadicea!*

That would explain all the other items, as druids were generally nomadic. They wouldn't accumulate many belongings, certainly not like the ones she could see here. But a queen ... most definitely.

"And while no one was certain where she was buried, there was a rumour — one of many — that Queen Boadicea might be buried near Stonehenge." *Considering her druidic connection, it was a possibility.*

Rhyll wished again she had her tablet to video all this.

Her thoughts now went to the green diamond itself, trying to fathom its relevance here, other than the colours. "Trees are green ... and brown ... and red, and many other colours, depending on species and season." She gave up on that reasoning. "Maybe not so much the diamond colour then, but perhaps the chakra is of significance."

She gave the design more scrutiny. It was difficult to judge, given the deterioration of the stonework and the lack of decent light, but there was the possibility of the slightest markings on the breastplate where the heart would be. *Either that or it's mould.*

Rhyll fetched the diamond from her pocket to place it in what she guessed was the right area. Her hand snagged on a dangling tree root, causing her to drop it. Before she caught it, the diamond bounced on the lid and fell inside the sarcophagus through the crack.

Shining the torch inside the crack, she could see the faint beam of light playing over the bones and rag remnants. As Rhyll moved the torch around, it briefly illuminated the skull. She hadn't really given it much thought, having seen many a skull in her time, but there was a difference. What surprised her was the amount of hair around the skull. She reached in and removed a few of the locks. She couldn't be sure in this light, but it had a reddish tint. A few strands went into her pocket for examination in daylight.

Squirming to a better angle she reached in, feeling the area. Rhyll turned off the torch, having briefly forgotten the crystal's glow would reveal its location, but before her eyes readjusted, she sensed it within the ribcage. Then it dawned on her. *Ribcage. Did the diamond just position itself?*

Rhyll moved back and waited a few minutes. Not the usual glow or pulsating, and there was no change in her surrounds. Nothing.

She'd grown out of being squeamish years ago, but truth be told, reaching into the ribcage of a centuries-old skeleton in a mouldy, dank tomb didn't fill her with joy. She crawled around to the larger crack on the other side, pushed her arm in again to retrieve the diamond.

What was that?

She could have sworn the sarcophagus moved. After pocketing the diamond she checked the base of the sarcophagus, where there was an accumulation of dirt and an outline, then a flat area.

It had *moved.*

Rhyll brought her legs up, braced her feet against the wall and pushed. The sarcophagus moved again. It was difficult work in the confined space. Sweating and panting with the effort, she managed to push it halfway. It was as far as it would go.

Roughly hewn steps descended into darkness.

"Why is it always underground?" she muttered as she knelt,

waving the torch and peering into the depths. The stairs went down about ten metres. After grabbing her case, she slid her legs over the edge and squeezed through the gap.

Shining the phone's torch downwards revealed rough and uneven steps. Rhyll descended the stairs, discovering another vault with a cracked, tiled floor. It was damp and musty — earthy — and a crystal platform similar to the one at Lake Titicaca almost filled the area.

I'm beginning to see a pattern here.

Rhyll looked closer as she played the light across the surface. It was covered in a fine layer of dirt and a couple of stone fragments. The crystal platform was almost identical to the other two: the body-shaped depression and the one niche, this in the chest area. "Heart Chakra." *Found you.*

She did a cursory walk around the perimeter, but there was little to see down here; it had a domed ceiling with a slumped section where some of the stone had fallen down, and the rough stone walls curving around the platform were bare and unadorned.

After removing the stone fragments, she slotted the diamond in the niche and undressed. She wiped down the dusty surface with her trousers, shook and folded her clothes and placed them on the edge near where her feet would be.

Rhyll climbed on and, with the briefest of shivers when her bare skin contacted the cool surface, she lay down. Like in previous occasions, the crystal platform began to glow and vibrate.

She woke up, refreshed. *No visions this time.* But the platform was pulsating and glowing.

"Two down, five to go."

With little more to do, she dressed and climbed out of the vault. Once back in the crypt, she decided to push the sarcophagus in place to prevent animals getting in and maybe disturbing the crystal.

As she moved around on the floor her eye caught the glint from a thick metal band. Carefully she teased it out of the built-up grime, dirt and rotten fabric. When she touched it there was a brief tingling, then a momentary dizziness. Rhyll slumped, waiting for the world to stop spinning.

So many new images coursed through her mind; many people in robes, white marbled halls, a battlefield with the dead and dying mounting around her, and she was holding a sword ... Visions totally different to what she had grown used to in her cave — these visions were harsh and bloody. She physically felt anger.

The band of metal was malleable without becoming distorted, and braided like a rope, and each end was sculptured into the figurehead of a lion.

Rhyll groped for one of the other diamonds in the case, knowing it would calm her. She rested until the images cleared and she was no longer disoriented. After replacing the diamond, she crawled back to where she'd found the items and picked up the sword. *Just like in the vision.* As with the sun-disc, the moment she grasped the hilt, the sword shimmered and appeared brand new, glinting in the torchlight.

She was no expert on swords but it did have a fine balance. It wasn't as heavy as she'd expected. *Made for a woman?* There was similar braiding on the grip, with a lion's head as the pommel. *The sword and torc were a matching pair.*

Rhyll decided carrying a sword around would attract too much attention, and reluctantly replaced it with the other items. *And it made me feel uncomfortable.* She shuddered at the violence.

Again, she wished she had her tablet. Sighing, she collected her case and quietly began the climb out. Pushing the case in front of her, Rhyll finally reached the surface, spitting dirt out of her mouth. As she breathed in the fresh air, her phone beeped several times before she could mute it.

The soldiers were still present. She couldn't see them, but could hear them. From the torches, it looked like they had split up to cover all sides of the woods.

If they'd heard her phone chime, they gave no indication.

The next thing she realised was the light filtering from the east. It was almost dawn! Looking at her phone, she saw it was 6:17am, and she'd missed several phone calls and as many messages.

She made sure her phone was muted before she texted a reply to Nala: *"Where are you? I'm near Stonehenge. Can't talk. Army close by."*

Rhyll sat, waiting for a reply. It was too light to attempt to sneak away; she didn't relish the idea of sitting here all day and there were still several chakra points to visit before anyone was safe.

Her phone vibrated. A reply message from Nala: *"Army seem friendly enough. They can bring you to us."*

Rhyll had to come to a decision: stay or go.

CHAPTER FOUR

RHYLL MOVED AWAY FROM THE ANCIENT OAK AND WALKED DOWN the mound. Looking back, she saw a faint aura now surrounding the tree trunk and spreading to the other trees.

She resumed her walk, pushing through the thick foliage and approached the nearest group of EV clad soldiers.

"Good morning." She stifled a laugh when they jumped.

They surrounded her immediately, asking inane questions: "Who was she? Where had she been? Why was she running? Didn't she know it was dangerous?"

With her bio-chip easily scanned, it seemed pointless to lie about her ID.

"Rhyll Ellis. Obviously, I've been in there all night. As for why I was running, why were you chasing?" These people were definitely military like those in the GHO, but she didn't recognise their insignia, an image of the UK surrounded by a helix circle.

"We've cordoned off the area due to the latest infection outbreak," one of the female soldiers said.

Rhyll shook her head in disbelief. "Don't you realise by now there is no actual infection? Haven't you been watching the news?"

"We're only following orders based on latest expert medical advice."

"What's in here?" a male asked, snatching the locked case from her.

"As you can see, it clearly states 'historical artefacts'. I'm sure you know, or your superiors do, that unauthorised tampering with it can cause a very costly and detrimental diplomatic incident."

"You open it, then."

"I don't have the combination—"

"Then what are you doing with it?" he asked.

"I'm just the courier." Rhyll pointed to the various national seals. "I think we should meet your supervisor, someone with authority to sort this out. You don't want to create an international political situation, do you?"

The female soldier that spoke earlier gave her a perfunctory frisk, finding her phone. Without too much rough-handling, Rhyll was escorted to one of the vehicles and they drove east in a small convoy. The soldier with the case sat in the front seat.

She chastised herself, belatedly realising the message she got from Nala wasn't sent by her friend. This group didn't appear all that friendly yet. "What corporation owns you lot?"

"We're Department of Infection Control."

"Do you know anyone in GHO?" she asked them.

They shook their heads, driving on in silence for almost an hour to a military base in Winchester. She was ushered into a long, two-storey building and placed in a cell with a barred door.

"Locking up kids now, are we? Should I ask for a phone call?" she yelled between the bars. "If anyone tampers with that case, they'll be sorry!"

"Our supervisor will deal with you shortly. You can do all your talking with her." The soldier closed the door.

"Rhyll? Is that you?" She recognised Nala's voice from somewhere along the corridor.

"Nala? What are you doing here?"

"After you left us at the crash site, this patrol from DIC came through to evacuate everyone. We drove off and tried to get around through some back streets but a drone spotted us. How did they get you?"

"From your text message." Rhyll felt stupid.

"What message? Where did you go?"

"I'll tell you later, once we're out of this mess. Is Dan here?"

"I think he's in another building — one for males."

After an hour Rhyll heard doors open and close, then footsteps getting louder. They stopped outside her door. After the sound of keys in the lock, the door swung open.

"Come with me," one of the EV clad female soldiers said. The ring of keys zipped back on a retractable line at her waist.

With her cell door left open, Rhyll followed another guard. The two of them escorted her back along the corridor, past the door she'd come in by, and deeper into the building. They went upstairs. This section was carpeted and wood-panelled, leaving the bare, cold concrete walls and floor behind. On the way, she saw other buildings and gardens through the windows.

The lead soldier opened a door halfway along a corridor and motioned for Rhyll to enter, closing the door behind her, leaving her alone.

The office was cold and bland with bare polished floorboards, empty and dusty bookshelves and floor-to-ceiling windows needing a clean. Again, the view from the window showed greenery and a soccer field.

On the trestle table in front of her was a monitor and a camera. On-screen she could see a woman in uniform standing behind her desk, a high rank from all the regalia she was wearing. There was a large window behind her showing the concrete expanse of an empty car park.

On-screen, Rhyll saw her case was opened and the items laid out.

"Rhyllien Ellis, is it?" the officer said.

"Who are you? What gives you the right to open the case?

Can't you see those official stickers? You have my friends captive here, so you're obviously aware of the authorised certificates we have."

"I'm Lieutenant Colonel Mayhew, the commandant of this facility. Neither the Brazilian Cooperative nor São Paulo University have any jurisdiction here. DIC makes its own rules."

"They're international clearances. You had no right. We didn't break any law—"

"We aren't the police, so we're not concerned too much with the law. What are these?" The commandant indicated the items. She casually picked up the prism for a brief look, then the sundisc.

"Ancient relics, as indicated on the certificate—"

"They look like tourist crap. Are these glass beads?" The commandant tossed the prism back onto the table with a thud.

"Obviously you're an expert on the matter. We should have come to you first. These items were declared at Customs, both in La Paz and Gatwick. That should be enough for you."

"Then why out this way and not the British Museum?"

A vague memory from many years ago came to mind. "Professor Ellis knows someone at Bristol University in antiquities. I was going there to get the contents verified."

"Who?"

"Why? So you can go harass him, too? Why are we locked up? What gives you the right to break into other people's possessions?"

"Maybe you're another one of these stupid wiccans that are starting to turn up? You lot can't do your rituals without approval. In medical emergencies, DIC have the power—"

"What rituals? Just admit you're a thug hiding behind a camera, behind a desk and a uniform."

"DIC have every right—"

"Yeah. That's what thugs say. Why are we being held?" she repeated.

"Your health and safety. You and your friends breached the quarantine boundary and defied the evacuation orders. We found you near Stonehenge. Why were you trying to get there? This superstitious festival for Samhain has been cancelled."

Rhyll shook her head. "You obviously know who I am, where I've come from, and I told you where I'm going. Do I look infected to you?"

"It is interesting. I have seen reports. Maybe it's you and your friends that are the ones spreading this disease."

Rhyll forced a laugh. "This all began last week simultaneously around the globe. We couldn't possibly have been responsible. How do you explain no infections in La Paz? No infections in Gatwick? Or on the plane over here with hundreds of other people, all sharing the same recycled air?" The obvious answer revealed itself. *Only when I'm stressed or threatened. The mine and São Lucas, Manaus — I was stressed and angry both times. Did I do that?*

Rhyll leant on the table as the realisation hit her.

The commandant kept talking. "We'll find the answers once we examine you—"

"You realise you're handling these objects without gloves. Maybe they're contaminated.

"We've sterilised and double-checked the contents."

"Perhaps I'm looking at a dead woman who's too stupid to know it."

"You certainly have a mouth and an attitude to match."

"Yeah. I get that way when my friends and I get locked up. Your best bet is to let us all go."

"Maybe we'll talk again once you get a civil tongue. Guard!"

The door opened quickly and the female soldier strode in. "Ma'am?"

"Take this brat back to her cell. I can't get a decent answer from her. Once the doctors arrive we'll start the examinations."

"Yes, ma'am." The soldier grabbed Rhyll's arm. Rhyll struggled with her briefly but the stronger woman slapped her away and dragged her out.

"I'm giving you one last warning. Let us go before you all

regret it," Rhyll yelled over her shoulder. The door slammed shut.

The stony-faced guard frogmarched her down the stairs. Rhyll had to walk quickly to keep her balance. "I meant what I said to your stupid boss. This will not end well for any of you. Are you as dense as her?"

The guard pushed her headlong into the wall. "Oops."

Rhyll twisted away at the last instant, and pain erupted as she hit the wall with the side of her head and shoulder instead of her face. *Looks like it's getting stressed-and-angry time again.*

The guard dragged her along. "Had enough?"

Rhyll waited a moment for some sign. Nothing.

"I was right," she continued to bait. "You are as dense as your boss. Do they train you to be this stupid or is it a natural talent? Maybe tablets?" As the soldier shoved her roughly, Rhyll pivoted abruptly, forcing the woman to run into her.

After the briefest of tussles, Rhyll was pushed to the concrete floor. "You're one insane brat. You must make your parents so proud," the guard jeered.

Rhyll gasped, as her arms and shoulders were jarred. "At least I know who mine are."

That remark got her a kick in the ribs.

"And that's for making us stay out all night in the fucking cold." Rhyll was then physically dragged in front of her open cell.

"What are you doing to her?" Nala called out. "Leave her alone!"

"Shut it or you'll get the same," the soldier called back, her face shield misting with the exertion. As Rhyll tried to stand, the soldier kicked her arm away. "You can crawl in."

On her hands and knees, Rhyll started crawling. As expected, she felt the force of the boot against her arse as the soldier kicked her inside.

"Maybe you'll learn to keep your trap shut." The door slammed.

There was a crack of thunder and the lights flickered.

Took long enough. Pushing through her pain, Rhyll smiled sadly. "Thank you."

"Bloody crazy bitch." The soldier swore as she stomped away.

Rhyll opened the hand holding the keyring she'd snatched when they tussled. She crawled to her bunk and rolled onto her back, breathing slowly. Feeling sorry for herself, she concentrated to remove the aches and pains in her backside, arms and ribs.

CHAPTER FIVE

"Rhyll?"

Rhyll woke up from her doze to the sound of thunder and rain.

"Rhyll?" She heard Nala's voice. "Are you alright? Answer me."

"Hey, Nala." She stood up and stretched, then moved to the cell door. The distant windows gave no indication of the time of day. "I'm fine now. Any idea what time it is?"

"No, they took everything."

"How long have you been calling me? I dozed off."

"About forty-five minutes, I guess. What were you thinking? You need to keep your mouth shut."

"It was necessary."

"Necessary to get beaten up? This isn't the girl I knew in Brazil." Nala sounded distant, perhaps several cells away.

"A lot has happened since then," Rhyll sighed. The corridor beyond was empty and silent. She reached through the bars, inserted the keys several times until she found the right one and the lock turned. Before she stepped out, Rhyll carefully checked the corridor. Sure enough, at each end was a security camera.

She'd only have a few minutes before the movement was

noticed. As she passed the next cell, she saw a robed woman sliding off her bunk. One look at Rhyll and she dropped to her knees, forehead to the floor and arms stretched in front. The same with the next two cells: each time there was a robed woman kneeling and praying. Nala was in the last one.

"Hey you." Rhyll surprised her friend sitting on her bunk.

"Rhyll? How ...?" Nala came quickly to the door as Rhyll worked at unlocking it.

"If you get them angry, they lose concentration. The dumber they are, the easier it is."

"You also get beaten up." Nala gave her a quick hug of relief when Rhyll pulled open the cell door. "How are you feeling?"

"Fine now. There are others in here." Rhyll moved back to the other cells and began unlocking them, Nala following.

"I thought I heard someone earlier. They must have been here before Dan and I arrived, but they didn't respond to my calls," Nala said.

In the first cell was a bruised woman, mid-twenties. The moment Rhyll appeared, she dropped back to her knees in obeisance.

"It's okay. We're not going to hurt you," Rhyll said softly.

"You are the blessed spirit of the One." She was looking at Rhyllien. "I see your aura."

"My name is Rhyllien, this is Nala."

"I am Arwen, and I thank you for releasing me." She grabbed Rhyll's hand and kissed it.

Rhyll pulled her hand away gently. "There's no need ... Pleased to meet you, Arwen."

"Did you find my sisters?"

"The two others? I believe so." Rhyll made her way to the next two cells, unlocking the doors. Arwen ran in to hug her sister, then they joined Rhyll and Nala at the last cell as it opened up.

"These are Damiana and Celeste," Arwen introduced them both.

"The blessed spirit of the One," they recited, reaching for her hand like Arwen had. Both of them also showed bruising from the guard's rough treatment.

"We should go before the guard realises I stole her keys." Rhyll turned to leave.

"If it was the blonde-haired one, she did this to us," Arwen stated.

Rhyll ducked across the corridor to the nearby exit. Looking out the nearest window, she could see dark clouds hanging in the sky. Combined with the mist, it made for a very dull and unpleasant day.

The five of them stared out the window. The inclement weather kept the people indoors. Anyone unfortunate enough to be outdoors had their heads down and under umbrellas. Some looked like they were coughing. No one here was in EV suits.

"Are we getting Daniel?" Nala asked.

"Not right away. If he's in a separate building, I doubt these keys will work there. He'll have to wait another hour or so."

"Another hour?"

"Maybe more, maybe less. So you reckon he's in that building over there?" Rhyll was looking directly across the road.

"I'm not sure. All I saw was they took me this way, and him opposite. It was dark."

"See those trees?" Rhyll pointed back along the road, which was lined with evergreens. Beyond, they could see a line of rooftops, obscured by the mist and sprinkling rain. "When it's clear, we'll make a run for those."

They opened the door and kept it ajar, looking out, waiting for an opportunity.

"Are you girls able to run?"

"We will do as you command, Great Spirit."

I'll take that as a yes. Rhyll hoped it was before someone saw them on the camera. She was surprised no alarm had been raised yet. *Unless they were too ill.*

Moments later, the street was clear of traffic.

"Let's go."

Rhyll led, Nala on her heels with the others as they sprinted along the footpath, crossed the road and threw themselves into the shelter of the trees. It wasn't thick coverage, but there was undergrowth to crouch behind if need be.

They paused to rest against the tree trunks, breathing heavily.

Still no alarm and no sign of anyone spotting them. Further along the road was an entrance gate, and just beyond the shrubbery behind them was a long fence of wooden palings. The rooftops they'd seen earlier were higher pitched and made of a different tile to the barracks.

"Don't the army like everything uniform? These will be civilian houses, then?" Rhyll asked.

"This is England. I'm not familiar with their customs other than afternoon tea, fish and chips, and warm beer."

"Pretty sad, a whole culture coming down to that," Rhyll chuckled.

"And it rains a lot too, but I can't blame them for the weather, and now that you mentioned food, I admit to being hungry."

"These homes are not part of this base," Arwen answered Rhyll.

They spied a house without a smoking chimney, apparently deserted, and edged along the fence until they found a spot where they could clamber over to sneak down a side path toward the street.

They were on a suburban street: red-bricked houses sitting shoulder to shoulder along both side of the street, all with small garden plots in front. Jack-o'-lanterns and other decorations were in some of the windows.

Hearing traffic and a car horn, they walked until they found the main street. A block later they reached the outskirts of the town centre with its shops, pubs and cafés.

"We must join our coven," Arwen said. "Will you join with us in preparing for Samhain?"

"As honoured as I am, not at this time. We have another friend to help."

"But how will—"

"Arwen, enough questions," Damiana spoke forcefully.

"The blessed spirit of the One will do as she desires. Sacred One, forgive her. Have we your blessings to leave for the gathering?"

"Gathering? Um, yes. Sure. Will you be alright?"

"With your blessing, we will endure."

"Oh. That's good—"

The three girls dropped to their knees, heads bowed.

Nala mouthed the words, "Bless them."

Rhyll took a deep breath, touching each of their foreheads as she spoke. "Beannacht ort féin agus ar do shinsir. Beidh grá ag máthair an Domhain duit go léir."

"So be it." The three women intoned. They got up after each kissed her hand and walked briskly down the road.

"That was ... interesting." Nala watched them go. "Was that the same as what you said in Amarete?"

Rhyll nodded. "But in Irish this time. No doubt they were the wiccans the commandant mentioned caught beyond the boundary."

"That's what I thought. And still living."

"It might be too soon, or they could be survivors like you and Dan." She wiped her face. "This standing around in the rain is going to get attention."

"And you can speak Irish now?" Nala asked, as the pair briskly strode into town. They could still see some movement, though it was subdued by the rain.

"Nope." Rhyll shrugged. "Though my grandfather is Welsh. Maybe I should have said "Bendithion arnoch chi a'ch hynafiaid. Bydd mam y Ddaear yn caru chi i gyd."

"Now you're just showing off."

Closer to the shops they saw the tables and awnings of a café.

"Hey, show-off, tell me what you got up to last night and I'll shout breakfast," Nala offered.

"Deal."

They stepped inside the nearest café — the bell chimed as the door opened — and found a table against the wall and near the fire. There were eight tables, all empty.

A plump woman came from the back, wiping her hands on her apron.

"Hello, loves. What can I bring yer? Got caught in the rain did yer, pet? You'd be wantin' somethin' warm then. We got pies of all sorts."

"Anything vegetarian?" Rhyll asked.

The lady's smile wavered slightly. "We got vegie pasties, or ricotta and spinach rolls. We got nothin' *vegan*."

"That's fine, the pasties and rolls sound great." Nala nodded. "Could we both have two of each, and perhaps two black coffees?"

"Comin' right up." She turned and headed back to the kitchen.

"So ... about last night?" Nala encouraged Rhyll.

Rhyll described her cross-country camel ride towards Stonehenge and ending up in the barrow instead, what she did with the green diamond, and her text messages when she climbed out.

"I don't know if I could handle crawling in and around a grave," Nala admitted afterwards. "Good work on finding the other chamber."

"It was more of an accident." Rhyll nodded her thanks. "Tell me what happened after I left you two?"

"We were interviewed by the reporters and the police. We told them we didn't know who the thieves were or what they were after."

"And the reporter?"

"Brody just wanted to know about you and where you got to. Who you were, how you helped the lion and why it didn't attack. Then DIC came through and moved everyone on because of the quarantine. They were expanding the roadblocks anyway. I think the police mentioned you, or they saw the news vid ... That's why DIC started scouring the countryside for you specifically."

"Well, the commandant broke into the case and has

everything in it. The cow." Rhyll stopped as their food arrived with two mugs of coffee.

"Don't know how yer can stand that muck," the lady said, placing the mugs down. "Hideous, but I guess yer not from around here. Ghastly business this quarantinin'."

"Are they going to empty Winchester?" Rhyll asked.

"Aye. They says they'll begin the push in a couple o' days. Nowt but trouble is wot's goin' ta happen."

"I think you should get out sooner," Rhyll advised her earnestly, but the woman chuckled.

"Me fam been 'ere for centuries. We be stayin'." She took the tray back to the kitchen.

The pair got stuck into the food quickly, neither having much to eat since their arrival, and Rhyll also had an appetite from her healing.

"You going to tell me why the beating?"

Rhyll swallowed. "You probably worked out this death wave turns up when I'm stressed, angry or injured. It happened at the mine, in São Lucas, and Manaus. So, unless you know how to defeat a bunch of armed soldiers … We need them to be incapacitated first."

"Incapaci— You mean dead? That's … harsh." Nala gave her a serious look.

"I'm being delayed out of sheer greed or ignorance. Under Lake Titicaca, I learned if I don't get to all the chakra points, *everyone* will die. And I do mean every man, woman and child — including you and me. But if I *do* succeed then those who can resonate with nature will survive. Any delay is going to cost many more lives that otherwise could be saved. The one saving grace about this is the diamonds are here; that means their healing influence will save anyone who is attuned to them."

"Like the natives in São Lucas." Nala sipped her coffee and made a face, almost gagging. "Instant coffee!"

Rhyll chewed more of the pasty, trying not to laugh. "The commandant spoke to me via vid-link. Did she speak with you?"

"No, not a word except from the soldiers. Why through the vid?"

"In case I was contaminated, I guess. She didn't seem too concerned for her people, though."

Nala shrugged. "When they become a high rank, the subordinates are nothing to them."

"Or they could be just natural arseholes."

"How long before we go back for Dan?"

"It usually happens within an hour or so after the lightning starts."

"Assuming this lightning *is* you and not just a storm. This is England in autumn."

"Had the lights been flickering before my beating?"

"I don't think so."

"We'll have to wait and see. You and I aren't able to free Dan and get the case back while the armed troops are breathing."

She cocked her head at a strange noise over the thunder and rain. She sipped some coffee and swallowed, sharing Nala's distaste for it. "Was that gunfire?" She looked at the clock on the wall. It had been well-over an hour since her beating.

Nala listened. "I can't hear anything."

"No ... it's stopped. I think we should head back after this."

When they finished, the lady didn't respond to their call. Nala left some cash on the counter and they made their way outside. Looking in one direction, there were some people seen going into or out of the shops, but they were at the other end of the village and little detail could be made out.

As they walked along the street, retracing their steps to the barracks, a car veered around a nearby corner and ploughed through a brick fence, coming to rest against the front wall of the house.

They both ran over to help. There was just the driver, a civilian, and it was clear from the blood and vomit he had already succumbed to the death wave.

Surprisingly, no one emerged from any of the nearby houses to assist or investigate the noise.

"Just like in Brazil," Nala observed.

Rhyll nodded. She was responsible for the deaths of these citizens. "I think the effect is happening faster."

Silently, they both made their way back to the army base. Just in case there were soldiers still aware enough to fire a weapon, they climbed the fence behind the house and hid in the bushes until they confirmed the area was safe. After several minutes of inactivity, they crept to the building where they believed Dan was being held.

It was a reversed layout to the building they were held in. They quickly found his cell.

"Good. I'll go and find some keys."

"Wake up, sleepy head," Nala called out to Dan as Rhyll jogged to the door at the end of the passage.

Dan sat bolt upright, looking dazed and surprised. He wiped his face, then slid off the bunk. "What are you doing here? How'd you get out?"

"As usual, the girls are here to help. Rhyll's getting the keys now." Nala filled him in on the recent developments. Shortly after, Rhyll returned.

"Hey, Dan." Rhyll waved through the bars, then proceeded to try the keys.

"Good to see you too. Where are the guards?" he asked.

"Most are dead, but some are lingering with other things on their mind."

"That's ... unfortunate."

"It's the way it is. If they left us alone ... maybe it would have been different. I'm coming to terms with it, harsh as it is."

"If it's like the other places, they would have died anyway." The cell door swung open. "Thanks," he said. "Where to now?"

A deep voice called along the corridor: "You would be doing me a kindness if you freed me from my cell also."

"There's someone else? I didn't hear him," Dan said in surprise as he followed the girls to the voice.

A tall man with long, wavy hair stood and approached; he had a tanned and weathered face. He bowed his head when he saw Rhyll. "My Lady, it is an honour to cast my eyes upon the spirit of The Divine One. I am humbled before your presence."

"Thank you, but no need. I'll get you out as soon as I find the bloody key." Rhyll flicked through them, eventually unlocking the door. "I'm Rhyllien, this is Nala and Daniel."

"Honoured to meet the companions of the Spirit." He nodded to them briefly. "Rhyllien, there is a power about you I have not seen before, only dreamt."

"I hear that a lot." Rhyll studied him for a moment. He had a wild look to his eyes and smelled ... earthy, but she sensed his calm. There was also a medallion around his neck — a triquetra in a Celtic ring, tied with a woven leather strip; she'd seen the design in her father's notes. "You're a druid, aren't you?"

"A druid?" Dan asked. "Are they real?"

The man stood straighter. "I certainly am." He inclined his head. "I am Keagan Thatcher. Young sir, I'm as much a druid as my predecessors, part of an ancient order devoted to the love of the land, sky and sea."

"Much like the shamans in Brazil," Nala added.

"They are involved at a deep level with the world around them and follow a path that respects and protects the natural world and its unseen power. They hold trees as sacred, especially oak. It's in my father's notes," Rhyll finished, then turned back to the druid. "We released three women earlier. I believe they are wiccans. Anyone you know?"

"Ah, good. I'm glad they are well. We were nabbed on our way to Stonehenge early last night," Keagan said. "But many more were successful."

"This would be for the preparations for Samhain? I nearly forgot the date." Rhyll turned to the others. "Otherwise known as Halloween; hence the decorations we saw in the town."

"You went into town?" Dan looked surprised.

"And a good festival it will be," Keagan continued. "You would do us all a great honour to attend with us."

"I have to get to Glastonbury Tor as soon as possible. Will

you be alright from here?" Rhyll stood at the threshold of the opened door.

"These soldiers ..."

"Are no longer a concern to anyone, at least not between here and Stonehenge."

"Ah. Then yes. I will be alright. I was born and bred in the area." He stepped outside, unperturbed by the rain.

Rhyll put a hand on his arm. "Before you go, I should warn you ... Have you heard of this death wave?"

"Death wave?" Keagan turned back.

"This supposed infection — the reason for the quarantine."

"Ah. Yes, I am aware of it."

"And it obviously doesn't bother you. What's your understanding of it?"

Keagan considered his words. "This 'death wave' is but another cycle of the Great Spirit. All living things including mankind are at *your* mercy. Some will survive, some will not. For those that pass beyond the veil, their spirit, their essence will continue in another cycle sometime in the future."

"Well, it's here now. You'll be pleased to know you're immune. I can't say how it will affect anyone you know."

"I understand, and it is a tragedy no doubt, yet a necessity. The cycle must continue." With that, Keagan bowed once more and left, striding boldly down the centre of the road towards the gate.

"I think I like him," Nala announced.

"Yeah. I'm sure he's the life of the party. When were you in town?" Dan asked from the shelter of the doorway.

"Having a bit of fomo?" Nala teased.

"We had to wait to be sure there was no obstruction before we could rescue you. Now we have to go find the artefacts." Rhyll started walking in the opposite direction. "I need to find a building — possibly two or three floors — overlooking a large car park."

The trio started jogging along the road, confident now none of the soldiers were in any condition to do them harm. The buildings either side of the road were almost identical: same brick, window frames and roof-tiles. Even the paths and gardens were more or less the same.

Further along, the gardens became more ornate; the hedges showing better maintenance and the buildings becoming more ostentatious.

"I reckon we're getting closer to the officer's mess," Dan pointed out.

To their right they saw a large expanse of bitumen.

Rhyll stopped to look over the area. "I'm pretty sure that's what I saw through the commandant's window."

"That's a parade ground, not a car park." Dan chuckled. "Which means this building here is what you're looking for."

It was only a two-storey building on a slight rise with the parade ground on a lower section of ground. Following the path through the manicured garden, they came to a building with a Georgian portico on a stepped patio. Double doors with glass panels opened to a long, polished wooden floor. The interior had an old wood and polish smell about it. Doors lined the wall to their right, and halfway along on the left was a carpeted stairway.

Rhyll went to the stairs and began going up, Nala a few steps behind, followed by Dan. Through the door to the first office, Rhyll saw the commandant collapsed on the floor. It wasn't a pretty sight. From the looks of the mess, with nowhere to go for help, she'd suicided.

"Wait there," Rhyll called back to her companions. Rhyll stepped inside and around the body. The case wasn't on the table as she'd hoped. She allowed her mind to relax, vanquishing all thoughts, then concentrated on the one thing they needed to find. An image of the case appeared in a locked safe inside the cabinet in the corner.

"Did you find it?" Dan called from the doorway, looking away from the body.

Rhyll was searching the desk top and drawers. "I asked you to wait!"

"Just trying to help." Dan was surprised at the rebuke.

"Didn't need it; didn't ask for it." She slammed a drawer closed and took a deep breath. "The case is locked in that safe. Want to check her pockets for the keys?"

"Not particularly."

"That's what you get for not doing as I asked."

"What's got into her?" Dan whispered to Nala. He bent down and started searching the commandant's pockets, averting his eyes from the grisly mess that was her head, and trying to avoid the worst of the blood and vomit.

"Rhyll caused these deaths," Nala whispered her reply.

"Hasn't she done all of them?"

"The first two events weren't her fault. Those deaths — the ones at the mine, São Lucas and Manaus — were all brought on unknowingly by the stress and anxiety she was going through. Remember my grandfather's words: 'It would be foolish to thwart her, for Gaia's wrath is never subtle, always fatal. Treat her well.'" Nala waved her hand. "She did this on purpose so we could all escape."

"Oh. I didn't know. Found them." He stood up, tossing them over to Rhyll.

She caught the keys and went to the safe, unlocked it and retrieved the case and checked the contents on the table. The sun-disc, prism and diamonds. "All here."

"I found these, too." Dan held up a car key and looked at the emblem on it. "I've always wanted to drive a Jag."

CHAPTER SIX

IT TOOK THEM ANOTHER HOUR OF SEARCHING TO FIND THE REST OF their gear locked in a storeroom down the hallway. Dan needed his camera and tablet with all his notes and latest report, as did Rhyll, and the phones were necessary as they held the numbers for Cataleya, Ileana, Benigno and Felipe.

"After what happened the other night, I think I should interview you," Dan suggested as they wandered downstairs.

"Interview me? Why?"

"None of this can be a secret anymore. The death wave is slowly moving everywhere — every continent has it, and pretty soon there will be mass panic when they realise nothing is stopping it. You're the only one that can make a change, yet we have so many hurdles to cross. By continuing in silence, we'll continue hitting hurdles. If we go public, we might get more cooperation."

"We'll probably just make more hurdles," Rhyll muttered.

"The more public we make it, the more interest you'll garner and possibly the more lives saved. Nala's grandfather laid the foundations with his message, so I think it's your turn."

Rhyll slipped her tablet in her pack. "We have an hour or so of daylight left. We should make a move if we want to get to Glastonbury."

"You realise there will still be roadblocks?"

"How about we see how far we get?"

Dan shrugged. "One benefit with the countryside being evacuated; it's not as if we won't find accommodation if we get stuck somewhere, and no traffic."

"That's two benefits, but as long as it isn't another night in a cell, I'll be happy," Nala added.

They searched for the commandant's car, which was parked around the back.

"Any particular direction?" Dan began setting the Nav.

Rhyll climbed into the front seat. "Just the quickest way to Glastonbury, I guess."

Dan punched the information into the GPS. "Says here the fastest route is going back along the A303. If there's going to be a roadblock that's where it'll be."

"I assume there are alternate routes?"

"Sure, several." Dan selected the other options. "A bit longer, but away from the main roads."

"Make it so." Rhyll chuckled at a memory, waving ahead. "Who's manning the roadblocks anyway?" Rhyll asked.

"If they're in the zone, probably droids. Remember the ICON pod in São Lucas? There could be armed pods on patrol."

"Let's be careful then." She watched as Dan set the controls to manual and moved off.

"I'll try."

"Why do you always do that?" Nala asked him.

"Do what?"

"You're in a fully automated car with millions of dollars of R&D behind it, and yet you revert to driving it yourself. Computers react far quicker than humans."

"These automatic cars were only starting up last I heard," Rhyll chimed in.

"In most developed countries there's infrastructure designed to run these completely autonomously. You don't even need to be in it to control it," Dan explained.

"Like the hoverpods?"

"Exactly. Once fully automated electronic cars were utilised, the number of serious traffic accidents dropped significantly."

"That sounds good." Rhyll nodded.

"And yet there are those that still persist in going to *manual*," Nala reproached.

"These things can still be hacked, or they have glitches. I reckon we're okay since we are the only car on the road, so no accidents."

"You heard him, Rhyll. If we crash, it's his fault."

Through judicial use of backroads and aided by thick fog, they got as far as Amesbury. During the drive, they were lucky enough to spot the blue flashing lights of several police vehicles before they themselves were seen. Quick thinking, along with harsh scrapes and dents when driving through a field enabled them to dodge detection until they found another road.

"An automated car wouldn't do that," Dan declared as he kept driving.

"Weren't we going to avoid the main road?" Nala pointed to the road-sign indicating A303 ahead.

"To be honest, I didn't think we'd get this far. Our alternate path was taking us to Salisbury. I'm not certain if it has been evacuated yet, but I knew Amesbury was, hence the detour. It's as good a place as any to stop." He nursed the car as far as he could within the town centre. "And I think I broke the car going through one of those fields. I'm losing power. I reckon I've damaged the power cell coupling."

"An automated car wouldn't do that," Nala parroted him as the Jag ground to a halt. She looked out the window at the quaint street and the nearby awning. "At least you found a pub. All is forgiven."

. . .

The Antrobus Arms was a very comfortable old guesthouse on the main road out of Amesbury. Since the area had been cleared the day before, the place was empty of guests — alive and dead.

"I guess the benefit in developed countries is word gets around quickly, so while there maybe mass panic, there are fewer deaths," Nala said, looking around.

Dan brought in the bags. "Or DIC are as efficient with cleaning up as they are in rounding everyone up."

"Guys, I don't want to sound like a princess, but we've not bathed for days. I'm going to find a shower." Rhyll collected her pack.

An 'emergency exit' map indicated the guest rooms were on the upper floors so they searched for the stairs.

Like the others, Rhyll found an empty room with an ensuite. She scrubbed herself thoroughly then afterwards took the opportunity to call her mother and quickly let her know of the latest happenings. By the time she came downstairs, the others had started preparing dinner.

"I owe you both an apology for leaving you like that," she said. "I saw the cameraman and police coming over and felt it would be a long tedious night."

"It was, then we got taken by DIC." Dan turned on the TV, changing to the local station with the news, muting the commercials.

"Did you get to find out who those men were that stole the case?" she asked them.

Dan shook his head. "Obviously they were the ones following us from the airport, but it's highly unlikely they chose us at random; they knew exactly what to grab. Not forgetting we were diverted from Heathrow at the last minute. Someone at Gatwick was looking, whether Customs or someone else. There was no indication of diamonds, but I'm sure ancient relics would be worth a lot of money to the right people. They only grabbed that case and bolted without even looking inside."

"Volaris is in the market for artwork and ancient artefacts; we know they'd stoop low enough to murder for it. And then there was those shooters in the mountains," Rhyll said.

"And by the lake," Nala added.

"Agreed. The two parties coming to mind are Volaris and ICON; Stradjek is after you and runs Volaris, we've dealt with ICON a few times too. We've been fortunate so far. I can only hope it lasts." Dan sat back turning to the news.

"I didn't know what else to do. How were those men?"

"One broke his neck. The other two were taken to hospital," Nala replied.

"And the animals?"

"DIC arrived before any of them could be rounded up. If they weren't still in the trucks, they were left behind. They moved us all along, even the police." Nala went to check on the dinner.

"Here's our news." Dan unmuted the TV and they listened to the latest updates.

With reports of the sickness coming in, the UK corporate authorities were declaring a state of emergency in both counties and expanding their quarantine area. Similar to Brazil, the death wave was moving in all directions relatively evenly, unaffected by wind or other climatic conditions.

All Somerset and southern Wiltshire were evacuated with the adjacent counties preparing for possible evacuation within the next few days. Where possible and to prevent too much congestion, they attempted to stagger the clearing of the populace.

"It's travelling so much slower here — which is a good thing — but I wonder why?"

Nala sat down to join them with a tray of soup as well as crackers and cheese. "How about this theory; chakra regions are naturally occurring, whereas those other areas are a sort of defence mechanism. Compare it to slow, deliberate action as opposed to swift retaliation."

"So in other words, don't piss you off," Dan surmised looking at Rhyll.

"'Her wrath is swift and lethal'," Nala repeated her

grandfather. "And here I was thinking he meant Mother Nature."

"In Rhyll's case, it's the same thing." Dan pointed. "Hey, Rhyll, you're on the telly."

On the screen, Rhyll was clearly visible on the other side of the truck. The lion was lying awkwardly on its side; Rhyll had her hands on it, talking soothingly.

They heard the voice over of the reporter, Brody Thurston. *"Who is this mysterious girl who fearlessly aided a lion in distress? Let's see if we can get a few words with her."*

"Animals can sense who will cause them harm or not," Rhyll replied to his question. *"He sensed I was able to help, so he let me."*

"Fascinating, but how did you know what to do?"

"I've been with wild animals all my life, freed them from traps or out of swollen rivers. Anyone could see his leg was bent the wrong way and he was in pain. He knew instinctively from my soothing voice I was helping. You just have to remain calm and confident."

As the reporter was about to ask another question, another voice drowned him out. *"Shit. Those guys are breaking into the car!"*

"Ha, some quality soundbites there, Dan." Nala reached over and ruffled his hair.

The camera swivelled around to see the BMW moving off, and Dan giving chase. By the time the camera turned back to the reporter, Rhyll was sprinting down the side of the trucks.

"Looks like the mysterious girl is fast on her feet too," Thurston was saying.

They saw a clip of the police, then the two protesting girls. *"Nah, the ginger weren't one of us. Looked like some rich brat tryin' ta look important. It's the Animal Liberation Front that deserve the credit for freein —"*

The image cut to the reporter. *"We'll keep you updated on further reports and see if we can find out more about this mysterious, brave girl. Brody Thurston, signing off."*

"You haven't told me what happened last night." Dan muted

the TV again when the news went to the sport. "Good work with the rhino ramming them, by the way."

"Thank you." Rhyll filled him in on what she told Nala earlier in the day. "So, if it's like Lake Titicaca, the influence of the green diamond is now spreading across the land. I also found a sword and a torc in the crypt. I put the torc on for a moment ... it *called* to me as soon as I touched it. I know it sounds weird. When I held it I had these flashbacks; images of warfare, blood and chaos. I was fighting soldiers looking like the Romans you see in those old movies."

"That *is* a new level of weird," Dan agreed. "Except for your revival after three decades of hibernation, or disappearing in a flash of light back at Lake Titicaca, or cuddling lions and jaguars—"

"I think you're being a smartarse." Rhyll scowled at him, feigning umbrage. "Nala, do you reckon he's being a smartarse?"

"When is he not?"

"Maybe I should only give *you* the details then?" Rhyll said to Nala.

"Would a humble apology from this mere mortal do?" Dan inclined his head.

"I guess for this *one* time." Rhyll then told them her idea of Queen Boadicea.

"You see, telling me these things can be beneficial to you too!" Dan went to his tablet and began a search. "How do you spell it?"

After spelling the name, Rhyll said, "That reminds me, I need to go back to the barrow and take pictures and a video to send to mum. I know it isn't Inca-related, but this is something that will eventually be studied — depending on who's around in the *aftermath*. I don't think we'll ever stop researching our history."

"I'll also need to find another vehicle tomorrow."

"Considering your driving history, perhaps a four-wheel drive this time."

. . .

The following morning, since the girls were still in their rooms, Dan ventured into the town after a quick breakfast and strolled to the caryard he saw when they arrived the previous night. Hearing a drone, he ducked into the nearest building to avoid detection.

Once the sky was clear he continued. Even after his time in Brazil, walking through a ghost town was an eerie experience. Dan came across the local Tesco supermarket, deciding grabbing a few supplies wouldn't hurt. The idea of looting did pass his mind, but then he considered by the time anyone came back here — and there was no idea when or if that would happen — it wasn't so much looting than utilising goods that would otherwise be tossed out.

With that logic and the simple fact the doors were unlocked, he found a trolley and wandered the aisles searching for any practical items they could use, like torches and walkie-talkies, and food that didn't need refrigeration.

The market was large, but Dan discovered he wasn't alone when he heard, then spotted, robed figures walking the aisles with baskets of goods — mostly frozen food and drinks from the looks.

He remained circumspect in his wanderings and loitered around the hardware and electronics section; he didn't approach them, and if they were aware of his presence he didn't know, but the group of four left before he did.

With his trolley, he left the store and continued to the caryard, noting the amount of real-estate agencies along the main street. He counted seven already. One in particular caught his eye. Going by the prices being charged, the size of the building, and the Range Rover in the car park designated 'Manager', they were doing quite well for themselves.

Again, the door was unlocked. "People were really rushed out of town," he mused. Leaving the trolley by the front door he wandered in, making a beeline for the manager's office. A quick rummage through the desk resulted in finding the car key. Minutes later, with the goods stowed in the back and no drone in sight, he returned to the Antrobus Arms, parking the car in the rear under the carport.

The girls were having breakfast and the smell of freshly brewed coffee wafted through the back door.

"One four-wheel drive as requested," he said as he walked in with his box of supplies. "Do you think what we're doing is looting?"

Rhyll looked up from her bowl of fruit salad. "Probably. I mean, we're not using force, and there's no war or riots ... but we haven't the rights to it."

"If I was doing it, I'd call it survival foraging." Nala started pouring the coffee for everyone. "But then, I'm not doing it." She gave him a smile. "I'll back you up if it goes to court."

"I'm so enthused with your support." Dan helped himself to another serve of breakfast.

"Then there's car stealing to add to the list of crimes," Rhyll added.

Nala sat and began eating, talking between mouthfuls. "And absconding from lawful custody, grave-robbing, smuggling diamonds, trespass, squatting ... I'm sure there's a long list of potential crimes a good prosecutor would come up with against all of us."

"Hey. We're not grave-robbing," Rhyll protested. "You're an employee of São Paulo University, I'm your associate and we're gathering artefacts and undertaking official archaeological research at the behest of Professor Ellis."

Nala gave her a high-five. "To the intrepid tomb-raiders."

"Forget I said anything. I'll change my identity." Dan kept eating.

"Mind you, being a member of this outlaw gang, I'm just as guilty," Nala added.

Dan nodded. "We should eat as much as we can. We have a bit of a drive ahead of us, and no telling where the next meal will be."

"I thought you foraged for food."

"Well, yeah. Snacks for the road; not real food." He finished his bowl and then put bread in the toaster. While it was toasting he unpacked the walkie-talkies and started charging them. "I got a set of three, in case we get to areas with no phone reception." He sat down after retrieving a new vidcam.

"Hey, now that *is* stealing," Nala teased.

Dan waved off the accusation. "It's for documenting your *official* research. I'm sure the university will cover the cost if need be."

"That's not how it works." Nala laughed.

"Is this for the interview?" Rhyll asked.

Dan nodded reaching over to butter his popped toast. "Once we get it charged and find a suitable location other than the inside of a pub."

"I'll leave it to the professional." Rhyll took her bowl to the sink then returned to drink her coffee. "Do I need a script?"

Dan shook his head. "No. I won't ask curly questions or put you on the spot. Simply tell us who you are and what's happening, and why — if you can. I'll splice in previous footage from Brazil and perhaps tack Vitor's message on the end."

"Then what?"

"I've contacts in various TV networks, and then there's my father and his contacts, and finally the tried-and-true method of getting information out to the masses — social media, YouTube — whatever it takes. I reckon we'd get world-wide coverage within an hour of going live."

"What about Volaris and ICON? I doubt they'll leave us alone."

"That's why going public is to your benefit. Too many people will know about you and what you're doing."

"Well, I guess it can't be any worse." Rhyll drained her cup.

Nala filled the vacuum flask with the remainder of the brewed coffee. "Too good to waste."

Other than the drone that began to follow them shortly after hitting the main road they drove unhindered to the barrow utilising the track the DIC soldiers made available when they ran down the gate.

Rhyll noticed a new vibrancy to the landscape as she hopped out of the car.

"We could have walked here last night." The barrow was only a few kilometres from the hotel. She pointed across the A303 towards Stonehenge. In the distance they could see the large group of people, many of them garbed in white robes gathered around the ancient monument. "That will be the druids and wiccans preparing for Samhain. I guess we could pop over. After all, they are immune like us."

"So they can't be too bad, you reckon?" Dan smiled.

There were several drones hovering over the gathering as well.

"Who do you think is controlling these drones?" Nala wondered. "Would it be DIC? The police? The military?"

"It could be news broadcasters. Another reason to go public, so they know what we're doing is on the up and up."

"Except the squatting, trespassing, and survival foraging," Nala reminded him.

"Exactly."

"I'm going back into the barrow." Rhyll unpacked her tablet and a newer, bigger torch. "It's cramped down there, but if you want to take a look for yourselves—"

"I'll wait for your footage," Dan replied.

Nala agreed. "We'll leave the tomb-raiding to the expert."

With a quick wave, Rhyll headed off.

"Don't forget to turn on your walkie-talkie," Dan called out. He turned his on while he thought of it. "Go to Channel 6."

Rhyll's senses still indicated the direction she needed to go and her second venture into the barrow was quicker in the daylight. She noticed the once dead tree was looking less dead, with the small green stems beginning to grow from its gnarly branches.

Once she crawled inside and climbed down the shaft, she pulled the torch and tablet from her pack and began recording, doing a slow circuit of the barrow, zooming-in to capture the detail of the sarcophagus and the items.

When she grasped the sword, other than the visions, a sense of wonder, wellbeing and confidence overcame her. With the sun-disc and prism, there was an instinctive belief they were critical for her needs; the sword and torc on the other hand, while powerful, were not. She put them both on the sarcophagus lid, and considered the other items. Dislodging some small stones something protruding from the accumulated grit and debris caught her eye.

Always curious, she reached for it. *What the hell is an ankh doing in medieval England?* Ankhs were nothing special. Depending on what you read, they were sun symbols, fertility symbols, and a symbol of life, eternal life and even afterlife. It was also believed the ankh dated back to 3000BC. None of this came close to answering why it was here in a druid barrow in England.

After taking a large amount of images, she popped the ankh in a pocket along with a couple of coins and more strands of hair to replace what the DIC soldiers took.

Pushing the sarcophagus aside, she climbed down into the vault and recorded the platform as she did a circuit.

Closing it up like she did previously, Rhyll continued to the surface, convincing herself her decision to leave the sword and torc was pragmatic. *I can't carry every damn artefact around with me.*

CHAPTER SEVEN

DAN AND NALA WERE SITTING ON THE TAILGATE OF THE SUV chatting when she emerged from the woods, and jumped in surprise.

"Let me guess, your dad taught you sneaking too?" Dan asked.

"You get that way when moving through jungles with the natives." Rhyll emptied her pockets and spent a few minutes cleaning herself up, using her fingers to rake the spiderwebs and dead leaves out of her hair.

"Imagine the tangles and mess if I didn't get my hair lopped off," she mused. "Oh, and there's this." She showed them the hair strands, coins and ankh. "It is red hair!"

"That reminds me." Dan picked up his tablet. "When I was reading up on Queen Boadicea, I came across some interesting coincidences; they agree she was both a druid and a queen, became a warrior after she and her daughters were gruesomely mistreated, and there's a rumour she might be buried near Stonehenge; plus she also had a mass of red hair."

"She was a Celt, the red hair is understandable." Rhyll perused the various tabs he left open. "So there's a likelihood the barrow *is* for Queen Boadicea?"

"Seems so. Boadicea was the only warrior queen to raise an army to attack the Romans with some success. It's also said she was ruthless with a Celtic shortsword." Dan reached around and scrolled to the pertinent article.

"That would explain these battlefield visions from when I held it. I wonder if she was buried near Stonehenge because of her druid connection? Mind you, druids normally cremate their dead." After a few minutes reading Rhyll swapped tablets. "Here's my recording of the barrow's interior."

Nala and Dan sat and watched the vid with interest while she poured herself a coffee from the thermos, answering any questions they might have. During the quiet moments she observed the crowd at Stonehenge with a faraway look in her eyes.

Once the recording finally ended, Nala got up and stepped in front of Rhyll.

"That's pretty creepy. Wouldn't catch me down there." She looked Rhyll up and down. "Your hair's one thing, but we need to fix up your appearance too before we head over to that festival, especially before the interview. Have you got any cleaner clothes? Your tomb-raiding has covered you in dirt. Not an image to impress."

"My appearance?" Rhyll put her cup down. "I'm not out to impress anyone," she grumbled as she dug out a cleaner blouse. When she stripped her old shirt off, Dan abruptly swivelled away and grabbed his camera and decided to shoot pictures of the grove and the distant gathering at Stonehenge.

Nala winked. "Do you want to influence as many people as possible?" She fine-tuned Rhyll's blouse fit. "Rightly or wrongly, some people tend to look at what the person looks like before they decide to listen—"

"They'll die if they don't."

"But if they're not listening, they will miss your message entirely."

"They probably deserve it."

"Harsh, but true. Nevertheless ..." Nala undid a couple of

Rhyll's buttons.

Rhyll looked down. "So it comes down to cleavage?"

"It normally does. You've not been shy before." Nala shrugged. "What do you think, Dan?"

"I think ..." he turned to look. "I think I'll be Switzerland."

"Switzerland?" Rhyll quizzed.

"I'm remaining neutral."

"I think he's scared." Rhyll folded her old shirt and tossed it in the back of the car.

"This reminds me of a certain discussion in the Erdany mine cave; I'm not about to discuss bodily attributes of a teenage girl." Dan packed his camera. "And you *do* control lions."

"This is true." Rhyll quickly checked her reflection in the side mirror. *Meh.*

"One more thing." Nala picked up the ankh and after another cursory look, pinned it just above the lower buttonhole. "There, made it into a flashy brooch. They have an excuse to look now."

Dan coughed. "Are we ready to go then?"

"As ready as we'll ever be." Rhyll climbed onto the back seat.

· He turned the car around and followed the signs to the official entrance and in a few minutes they were at the tourist centre car park, but it was empty. The grounds encompassing Stonehenge were surprisingly large as it included many other barrows and ancient sites of historical interest. A gate marked 'for emergency use only' lay smashed and broken, bits strewn on the roadside. In the distance many parked cars were visible on the grass.

"Someone else drives like you," Nala quipped.

"I'll assume nobody wants to walk." Dan drove over the gate remnants towards the distant cars.

A crowd of people noticed their approach and came over to meet and greet the new guests. Although many were wearing white robes, there were also quite a few in furs or a mixture of clothing. Headdress was common whether it be a simple hat or cap, but a few antlers or horned helmets could be seen. Face-painted children scurried about chasing one another.

"Be on your best behaviour, Daniel," Nala cautioned.

"What did I do now?" Dan protested defensively.

"And tone down that weird-shit-o-meter of yours. Some people take this seriously. Here comes Keagan."

Rhyll recognised the druid from the Winchester cells striding towards them with a group of white-robed men and women.

"Well met, Divine One," Keagan called as Rhyll stepped out of the Rover.

After the briefest of time, the nearest druids bowed low, some dropping to their knees. Mutterings of 'queen', 'Boadicea', and 'great spirit' were heard. Like a wave, others further back followed in kind chanting in Gaelic.

"What are they saying?" Dan whispered.

"Some are entreating forgiveness, or beseeching wisdom, or for me to share the blessing of the light ... chants and prayers for surviving when so many they know have died or fled."

"Divine One, you honour us with your blessed presence," Keagan spoke as the voices subsided.

"Keagan, it is I who is privileged to meet with you again." Rhyll raised her voice. "Beannacht ort féin agus ar do shinsir. Beidh grá ag máthair an Domhain duit go léir." Rhyll repeated the Gaelic greeting from the other day.

The crowd muttered in surprise, nodding to each other in appreciation.

"Please rise, good people."

Slowly the crowd rose to their feet, soft mutterings swept across the area. Some children pointed only to be scolded softly by the adults.

"Why is she speaking like that?" Dan whispered to Nala.

"Shh."

Keagan inclined his head with Rhyll's compliment. "Will you be staying with us for the festivities and for Samhain tomorrow?"

"It would please me to be able to say yes, but we were but passing on our way to Glastonbury Tor. Out of dire necessity, I will have to decline your offer. I see you have caught up with your friends." Rhyll nodded to Arwen, Damiana and Celeste. "But can you tell me how everyone came to be here?"

The death wave had already spread over a large area before she managed to get the diamond in place, and it would have taken days to expand to encompass any of the surrounding villages.

"Many of our people were evacuated several days ago with everyone else. As you know, Divine One, some of us were caught dallying.

"When I witnessed your return to us, I knew it would be safe for us and called them all to return. Some didn't make it through the lines, but as you can see, many of us did, and many more will be making their way. Thanks to you, we have been fortunate in our reunion." He bowed again. "May we offer you refreshments for your travels? We have ample."

"We would be delighted to partake in your bounty." Rhyll bowed her head, turning slightly to look at Dan. "A hearty meal before our journey would be a boon."

"It pleases us greatly." As Keagan raised his arm in invitation, the crowd parted swiftly.

"Saying no would be an affront," Rhyll whispered to them as they were escorted to the pavilion. Dan looked sick already at the amount of food.

Trestle tables ran the length of the pavilion, loaded with various fruits, breads and other produce. At each end, groups gathered around the bonfires, drinking and spilling their wine and mead while singing and dancing got underway.

"We have been graced with a good season and bountiful crops," Keagan was saying to them.

"Bountiful crops? I saw some of them *survival foraging* at Tesco's too," Dan muttered to Nala, who elbowed him in the ribs.

"My good friend Daniel was just saying how he's barely surviving having missed breakfast this morning."

"Excellent, my lady. Preston, make sure this good man gets his fill."

A young lad nodded. "As is your will, Master Keagan." He started loading a plate with cheese, breads and fruit slices. "Would sir like a wine with that?" he asked Dan.

Dan nodded, his stomach churning already at the sight of the loaded plate. "You're nasty and cruel," he whispered to Nala.

"Eat up, you don't know when the next meal is coming." Nala winked. "Think of what Rhyll's going through."

People with plates of delicacies for the Divine One were lining up for the chance of meeting her.

Once the special guests were eating and drinking, the others joined in the feast. After watching him valiantly struggle with his plate, Nala took the plate off him with a sympathetic grin. "Maybe you should get ready for the interview? I don't know how much more food she can handle."

"Interview. Yes of course. Very important." Dan left the pavilion while Nala picked at the remainder of his food.

Once Dan found a spot with good light and the daunting Stonehenge as a backdrop, he set the vidcam on a tripod. As he did a final check, a crowd began to gather, stopping at a distance so as not to interfere. Rhyll came over shortly afterwards looking nervous.

"You've got a bit of sauce." He motioned her to wipe her mouth. "When we start, I'll introduce myself, talk a bit about you and then go to you. Nothing I ask or say will be new. And don't worry, we aren't 'live', so I can do edits before putting anything online."

Rhyll licked her lips in apprehension as Dan moved her to the precise point he wanted her. "Talk to me if it makes you feel more comfortable, ignore the camera."

Nala came over, standing nearby. "Remember this will save a billion lives. Where's the defiant redhead that hassled armed soldiers, or who wrapped her arms around a lion?"

Rhyll smiled, nodded and composed herself. "Ready."

Dan stood beside her and activated the vid with his remote.

"Dan Dobson here and on this night, 31St October, I'm talking to Rhyllien Ellis. Some of you may recognise the name from previous reports. This is the young girl who recently saved a lion in distress; the girl who died thirty-five years ago; and the girl who is on a mission to save as many lives as possible around the world.

"You may scoff at these claims, but I'm here to tell you I have been with her since her awakening, and according to numerous tests by the GHO, her DNA is a 100% match to the missing child of the reputable Professor Ken Ellis, murdered in 2021. I have personally witnessed this girl do amazing and impossible things — and she's here now to do much more. Rhyllien, please tell us your story."

"I don't want anyone to die, but sadly many have, and many more will in the coming months. You've seen and heard reports of the death wave — this *sickness* the corporations tell you about. It's on all continents and is slowly spreading. The same corporations will tell you everything that can be done, is being done. They are lying to satisfy their shareholders and have absolutely no control over this whatsoever. This is why they are evacuating those affected areas in the vain hope they will find a remedy before many more die.

"I can tell you they will fail. I have seen it in other countries."

"Some might say God sent you to punish us for our sins?" Dan said.

"What is god? An all-powerful omnipotent being; the creator of all?" She shrugged. "Call it what you will, Gaia, Mother Nature ... it *simply is*. Just because it doesn't conform to your belief system is irrelevant. Look at what's happening around you; everyone that has died because of this death wave spent their life believing they were separate to nature, that mankind is somehow above it all.

"The only concern of Mother Nature is the Earth's survival and *all* its creatures, and mankind is but one of millions. For far too long Earth has endured the never-ending wanton destruction of the environment for wealth, greed and power. Now the Earth says no more!"

"Is there any hope? Do any of us have a chance?" Dan asked.

"There's always hope. Look around you. There are almost a hundred earth-loving people here in the restricted area. Mother Nature isn't cruel or vindictive. Like any living entity she simply wants to survive and wants all her creatures to as well. She will do what she can to succeed. You can all do this too. Reconnect! Understand mankind is no better or more important to the environment than a rodent, birds, insects, fish, or the trees. Acknowledge your place. Live in harmony with your environment and stop destroying it for personal greed and power."

"You're saying the hippies were right?"

"The hippies, the greenies … anyone who loves nature and understands their place in it has a better chance of surviving; they could be avid gardeners, naturalists and environmentalists … is Greenpeace, Sea Shepherd or World Wildlife Fund still about?" She continued at Dan's no, "and any of the many other environmental groups who are true in their beliefs — not just trying to get kudos, or for tax reasons. Behind me is the local group of druids and wiccans; lovers of all nature can provide, behind them is unmistakable Stonehenge. You are told this area is under quarantine by the Department of Infection Control because of this death wave. How is it we are surviving? Simple. We adhere to the belief nature is part of us and we are a part of nature. If you have no connection — find one. If you work for a corporation that's raping the resources of the earth; stop or die.

"You might be thinking this as some conspiracy theory or superstition. Look at what's happening in Brazil, in Egypt, here in the UK, Mount Shasta in California; none of your corporations has a clue. My task is to minimise the death toll."

"Some might say you are the cause of this. This death wave wasn't here until you appeared."

"Ask yourself who is saying it and to what purpose? Maybe I appeared *because* of this? I can only help those who want to be helped. If I'm successful, then there'll be survivors; if I fail, *all* of mankind — every woman, man and child will perish — leaving the land free for every other creature. The Earth will continue quite well without any of us."

"How long have we got?"

"I don't know how fast the death wave is moving. Time is of the essence; the longer I take, the more needless deaths there will be. I'm sure someone out there has crunched the numbers and will know. Ask them. Put up a doomsday clock on every website because it's happening. It's very real. You can't hide from it; running will only delay the inevitable. I suggest everyone who wants to live put all your energies in adapting."

Dan turned off the cam. "That's it. I'll edit some of it, splice in file footage of some of the things we've already seen and Vitor's message. I'll send it to every news agency I can, including my father's Nexos magazine. He can push it through his channels."

"Thank you, Dan." She gave him a relieved hug. The gathering chuckled and applauded. They both parted, faces reddening.

Nala put an arm over her shoulder. "Rhyll, you can't do much more. You've told them what will happen and how to avoid it. The rest is up to them."

"What if this all goes wrong?"

"You'll be far too high-profile; a personality to be reckoned with. If anything happens to you, they'll be clamouring in the streets, rallying by your side."

"At least someone's sure. I think I need a drink." They wandered to the pavilion. Two young girls, each with a band of woven flowers in her hair, came over with glasses of punch. A crowd gathered and Rhyll was swept away with them.

"It's just weird when she speaks to them; it's as if she's someone else; not like a sixteen-year-old girl," Dan said to Nala.

"Maybe not a different person, but a spirit of some sort? What she's gone through, what she's done, is doing ... will do ... is not normal for anyone let alone a teenager. After what you've seen, you of all people should understand that."

"I do. It's amazing and impossible ... I just feel uncomfortable about it."

"After she came out of that barrow she seemed different. *That* was creepy."

"Do you think something influenced her down there?"

"I don't know." Nala sighed. "We have to trust whatever it is she's going through is for the ultimate betterment of the world. None of what you or I think matters. We have to stick with her, support her."

"Oh, I have no doubt about that. I'm here, no matter what." Dan finished his glass and walked around with the camera to record some of the festivities, a retinue of children in his wake. After about thirty-minutes, he was about to pack up, when there was a roar, followed by screams and yells of fright.

The gathering were running from the north end of the pavilion in a panic. With camera still in-hand he went to look for Rhyll and Nala.

As the crowd surged by him, the lion and lioness from the truck incident could be seen trotting towards the pavilion. Nala found him as Rhyll walked calmly out to meet the approaching animals, her arms low and palms flat. She was talking, but too soft for them to hear clearly.

Nala nudged him. "Know how to work that thing?"

"Shit." Dan brought the vidcam up and began recording as the lions slowed and sauntered towards Rhyll.

The druids behind gasped as the lioness reared up and put her massive paws on Rhyll's shoulders. Rhyll buried her head in the animals neck while giving it a hard rub. She was almost bowled off her feet when the lion nudged her for attention. When the lioness dropped back to the ground, Rhyll crouched and roughed the lion's mane. She spent several minutes doing this before the two massive animals sauntered off towards the road to the south.

As Rhyll walked to Dan and Nala, the druids flocked around her, touching and praising her for her prowess and bravery.

Keagan, being the head druid, said a brief prayer in his deep, resonant voice.

CHAPTER EIGHT

TYRONE PACED BACK AND FORTH WAITING FOR THE UPLINK TO THE moon base named *Inspiration*. Despite all the work and research, his grandfather's *osteogenesis imperfecta* hadn't improved, and with ageing, it would only deteriorate.

Having no children of his own and losing his father as a child, Tyrone was going to make sure he didn't lose his grandfather and determined to put all his resources into his wellbeing for as long as he could. And considering the brittle bone disorder could be passed on, there was no guarantee he didn't have it. Regular testing so far had been inconclusive.

And there was always the cryogenics option.

It was his idea to house Viktor on the moon, where the reduced gravity would at the least give him some comfort free of the mind-numbing painkillers. His grandfather flatly refused to live in an orbital.

"It's a tin can in space. I want ground beneath my feet, whether it's ground on the Moon, or even Mars," Viktor had fumed.

The monitor flashed to life. First there was a blank white screen, then snowy static and finally the image resolved into his grandfather reclining in a motorised device part-hammock, part-chair.

"High Opa. How was the trip up the space elevator?" Tyrone asked. It had been three days since he sent Viktor up the space-lift. "Any ear-popping or vertigo?"

"I was unconscious most of it — painkillers and all — but I'm in Inspiration now. This one-sixth gravity is so revitalising, I'm virtually pain free. But, enough about me; what's the progress your end?"

"Not so fast. You can at least show me around the place; we're paying enough for it."

Viktor grabbed the camcorder and turned it around to face out. The 'chair' he was in swivelled and began gliding around the unit. "Obviously, the living area." There was a couple of modular chairs for able-bodied visitors with a table in between. Along one wall was a series of long windows showing the moonscape beyond. Viktor let the cam record the moonscape for a few minutes. The opposite wall showed more of the complex as it spread out. "I'm on the third level at the end of a hab-module." He moved into a short corridor. "Then there's the bedroom with ensuite, and the entrance."

"What about the cuisine?"

"For most inhabitants, there's the central mess area where they have normal gravity, but considering my condition, we have a dispenser here. I'm told I can get a la carte deliveries if I choose. It's almost better than on Earth." Viktor stopped adjacent to the window and repositioned the cam. "Now, quit stalling and tell me about your plans."

"I've been going about this the wrong way all along. Full-on frontal attacks are more detrimental to us. I've been thinking of getting her to do our dirty work instead and remove our competition."

"I gather your last plan failed? How do you propose to go about this next idea?"

"There's a pattern in this death wave. Sure, it spontaneously appeared in seven other locations around the world about the same time she turned up, but there are a few anomalies; whenever this Ellis girl turns up, another one appears."

"That would give credence to this message that native witchdoctor was spouting, Gaia wrath and all."

"Exactly. Looking back on it, in all those situations she was angry or under stress." Tyrone counted off the times. "At the mine and São Lucas, she was slapped around and imprisoned, at Manaus her mother was almost killed. From the reports I get, she was shot at near Lake Titicaca. Plan B — we don't actually attack her, but we'll take these diamonds. We can then send one at a time to our competition and give her their locations. She'll be forced to retrieve it; they'll of course try to keep possession of it. She'll get pissed off and hey presto, death wave ensues and no more competition. Then I send out the next diamond."

"I believe we're onto plan C — but what if they decide to simply kill her instead?"

"There's a risk I lose a diamond, but get to keep the rest. By now everyone knows what would happen if she dies. I'll even remind them of the dire consequences."

"And the-se diamonds—" The screen pixelated as a spurt of interference affected the transmission." —ho-w do y-ou expe-ct to pro-o-o-cure thethehemm..."

Tyrone swore, waiting for the static to fade. "The silly minx is plastered all over the TV. She's made it clear what her goals are and where she is. Facial recognition should pinpoint her whereabouts if we lose track of her. Once we grab the diamonds, she'll be told what to do — and the consequences if she disappoints."

"Apparently the death of all civilisation on Earth."

"Well, that too, but I meant the immediate consequences of failing *me*. I'll have her friends locked up; they'll pay for her failures."

"You can do this?"

"Sure. When I know her exact location I'll organise something, a gas drop if I have too and put the whole fucking town to sleep. A few of the lads will pop in, grab her friends and the gems and leave a phone. Then I'll call her and tell her the good news."

"Pop in? If I understand the talk of this death wave, isn't that a suicide mission?"

"We don't know how long before it takes effect. All the cases we do know had been in there for hours, but we'll try to nab her outside the zone if possible. I'll tell them to be as quick as they can — in and out. They'll be fairly compensated for the risk."

"Assuming you find someone foolish enough to try, when do you envisage this happening?"

"My sources believe we can act within a day or so. She's in the south of England at the moment and we're trailing her with a drone."

"If she's in the UK, how do you propose to guarantee her getting to where she needs to be — assuming it's these chakra points they're going on about?"

"I'll supply her with a top-of-the-line AI pod to get her where she needs to go. No more airports and customs to worry about."

"So, you're planning on taking over a billion dollars' worth of diamonds, then giving them away to our competitors *and* risking an expensive pod?"

"It's a worthy risk. As far as giving the diamonds away, we'll be rid of all competition and we'll soon have a monopoly in the space mining business. That loss will be recouped in a month."

Viktor grimaced as he shifted position in his chair. "What happened at the airport? I was in transit and heard later that turned into a fiasco."

"Last-minute changes due to the bloody English weather. Her flight was diverted to Gatwick. My man on the ground had to think quick and called in a few local lads. They blew it. His job now is to finish them off for their failure."

"I tr-ust you'll kee-ep me in the lo-oop?"

"Of course — assuming signal reception allows. Now, do you want to go through the other reports?"

"What is there?"

"A list of Earth assets to sell-off; asteroid mining businesses

— new start-ups and those ripe for a take-over; progress-report for our Mars bid; costings for freight and sundry fees—"

"How about sending it to me in a packet. I'll read it at my leisure — I have a lot of that here."

"Not a problem. Enjoy your a la carte."

"Until next time."

Tyrone looked at the blank screen for a moment. His next step was to decide which of his competitors should be on his hit-list. Going by what was happening on Earth, his priority should be those with off-world interests. They were the future threat.

"I am so glad that's over and done with." Rhyll sighed in relief when they finally left Stonehenge. While something inside her revelled in the idolisation, her gut said differently; it wasn't like her. She was the wild tomboy that could spend days in the forest without meeting another human; just her and the animals. *What happened to that carefree girl?*

"I thought you loved all that ceremonial stuff," Dan was saying breaking into her inner thoughts. He had been queasy for a while with the consumption of far too much food.

"I'm thrilled they're all still alive but one can only take so much of this bowing and scraping. It isn't for me. I love nature for all it is and can do, but not this idol worshipping. I'm much more comfortable crawling through a dark crypt or jungle than hob-knobbing it." She watched the passing countryside in the early afternoon sun.

Dan started the car. "So, we're off to Glastonbury Tor?"

"At this stage, or, like Stonehenge, it might be somewhere nearby. I'll know when I'm closer."

"We have just under an hour to go." Nala studied the Nav.

"Do you know of any roadblocks between here and the tor?" Rhyll asked.

"Not from what I heard on the radio earlier; it's all clear in between. The roadblocks are much further out."

"If the region is deserted, how are they getting updates?" Nala asked.

"No doubt some of the drones are giving feedback; there are also satellites and there's always the motorway traffic cams." He pointed to a small box, mounted on a high pole, which had a transparent dome at its base.

Even in winter, driving through the rolling hills of Somerset was pleasant, its lush green meadows grazed by black-faced sheep and a smattering of cows. Dan and Nala used the time to talk about the minor things they'd missed over the years, but there were occasional reminders—like the drones—that *somebody* was interested in their progress.

"Almost there," Dan said during a gap in their chatter.

They could see the tor in the distance with the iconic St Michael's bell tower at its peak.

"Those drones are still following us," Nala noted when she glanced out the window.

"*Those drones*? We have more now?" Dan leant forward, craning his head to look up through the windscreen.

"I can see at least three, but you should concentrate on the road," Nala advised as the car veered onto the shoulder. "Or go to auto."

Dan corrected his steering. "Rhyll, once we get there and while you're doing your thing, I'll get that vid sent out."

"How soon do you think it will gain attention?"

"Meaningful attention from corporations and governments? I've no idea, but you'll be everywhere on social media within an hour, you'll go viral; no pun intended." Dan slowed as they reached the township and narrower streets with some buildings almost to the curb.

Rhyll motioned to stop.

They got out and looked around at the quaint village. The entire town was empty; not a soul in sight.

"Doesn't look like there are any druids here yet," Dan stated the obvious, looking at the nearby hill.

"Maybe they're all at Stonehenge," Nala suggested.

Rhyll walked around the car slowly, paused, then moved off again. "I'm sure it's very close." She sensed the increasing strength with each step.

"Very close" turned out to be less than fifty metres from the parked car.

Dan read the sign. "The Chalice Well, otherwise known as the Red Spring or Blood Spring. Is this it?"

"Everything says *yes*." Rhyll walked into the garden car park, following her senses, whereas Dan was reading the directions from a slightly crumbled and weathered brochure left in a box near the entrance.

Somewhere inside one of the buildings they could hear recorded flute and harp music. Nala followed Rhyll, who was absorbed in the peaceful ambience.

"If you stay with Rhyll, I'll get this interview uploaded and make use of the great signal. I'll be in the tearooms just over there." He pointed.

"Don't eat all the scones." Nala followed Rhyll who was strolling under a long pergola of wisteria. The path was layered in fallen leaves and at the end was a small set of steps. The stairs were part of a series of tiers going to the top of a rise. Gardens surrounded the path and the sound of trickling water was prominent. Nala soon discovered a small but steady watercourse meandering through the gardens; there was a reddish tinge to the base and sides of the runnel.

Rhyll stood by a low well in a paved cul-de-sac on the next level. The opening had a wooden cover with an elaborately sculpted inlay of bronze. She examined it; tracing the design with her fingers. The lid was hinged. Rhyll lifted it up without effort, then knelt beside the opening, a look of deep concentration etched on her face.

Nala sat quietly a few feet away, silently watching and waiting. She could sense something too.

After a short period, Rhyll removed the indigo diamond from her pocket and simply dropped it into the well. A minute later she stood up, closed the lid and joined Nala on the seat.

"That's it?" Nala looked surprised.

"I think so. I hope so. The image *was* in a vision. It could be very tricky to retrieve it if not, but it felt right. There's no manual on how these things are done — just a feeling if it's right or not." She studied the surrounding gardens. "I thought each site was going to be similar."

"You mean underground with a crystal bed?"

"Something like that."

"Perhaps it's because the third eye chakra moves every hundred and fifty years, whereas the six others are permanent?"

"I hope so. I guess we'll have to wait and see."

Nala followed her gaze. "Are you waiting to see if it changes like it did in that grove at Stonehenge?"

Rhyll nodded. "Mind you, I must have fallen asleep. It had only turned to dusk when I entered the barrow, and it was dawn when I came out."

"Let's give it more time and see how Dan's going with his upload of the interview. You've done what you could here, we may as well be cosy."

The pair sedately walked along the path. Five minutes later they entered the tea rooms. Dan was glued to his tablet, cold coffee beside him, and didn't look up when they sat either side of him.

"Did you save us any scones?" Nala nudged him.

"Look at this! Over a thousand hits already." He pointed to one of the many windows he had open on his tablet. "I sent it to my blog, my father and every news source on my list, as well as every social streaming site I could find."

"You have a blog?" Nala laughed.

Dan frowned at her. "I don't get on it much, but it's a permaculture page."

"You did permaculture?" Rhyll asked, surprised, looking at his page. "You realise that's what probably saved you? Learning and understanding our connectedness with the environment."

"I had wondered at that too." Nala winked. "Not that I'm complaining … yet."

"I did the theory years ago via correspondence, but being on the road so much couldn't really get to do the practical side of things ... but I shared the information I found to others.

"By the way, I was right earlier, your story is going viral. You're famous." He pivoted the tablet for them both to see clearly, and enlarged the screen. "I sent it to Brody Thurston too, that reporter from the other night. He saw firsthand what you did and with his UKTV connection, has a bit of kudos in the European media circuit. He can push it much further."

"And you added the clip of the lions earlier today.

"A golden opportunity to prove you are nature's emissary." Dan nodded.

"I see you managed to not edit out the cleavage." Nala laughed at Dan's discomfort and blush.

Rhyll spent time reading through some of the comments while Nala grabbed cups of coffee and cake. "Apparently there's no scones left."

"They were stale anyway," Dan said in his defence. "I did you both a favour."

Nala joined them looking at the various sites. After they finished their drinks, Rhyll suggested a visit to the tor before it got dark.

Up close, the bell tower was an imposing piece of architecture. Dan huffed behind Nala and Rhyll as they traipsed up the steep path.

"This tower may not be tall or in the best condition, but it's steeped in myth. However, chronologically, it has nothing on the Incans or the civilizations dating thousands of years before them," Rhyll explained.

"Hey! We could have driven up around this track." Dan pointed to the narrow trail on the side of the hill.

"You realise it's not for vehicles?" Rhyll laughed. "The labyrinth, or maze, was a ritual spiral believed to be for pilgrims for contemplation. Possibly an opportunity to reach enlightenment."

"Fair enough. Still, it's a nice view." He wiped the sweat off his face, then wiped his hands on his jeans before he touched his camera.

"And if you follow the King Arthur myth, this is supposed to be Avalon," Rhyll continued.

"Wasn't Avalon surrounded by water?" Dan took a quick breather and admired the view of the many fields in the flat terrain below. While the tor was virtually clear, thick groves of trees dotted the surrounds, along with herds of cattle and sheep. He started snapping images of the tower and the countryside. Rays of the setting sun pierced the low cloud, making interesting effects on the stonework.

"The plains below us used to be a swamp, drained centuries ago, so this tor was an island a thousand years before ..." Rhyll paused. "Can you see that?" She pointed near the edge of town.

The others followed her gaze.

"Nope," both replied.

"It's faint, but there is a glow ... slowly spreading. I reckon it's following the flow of the spring."

"What spring?" Dan asked.

"Wherever the source of the well comes from, and wherever it empties."

"Another job done then." Nala clapped her on the back. "Three down, four to go."

"That's four more continents." Rhyll didn't look pleased at the prospect of so much travel.

They continued the remainder of the walk through the roofless stone bell tower. The interior had not been replaced in centuries, leaving a tall, hollow shell.

"I wonder why they didn't replace the upper floors?" Dan asked, bending backwards slightly to gaze at the top, then snapping a picture.

"I couldn't say. It's a bell tower. Maybe it was only a narrow belfry up there," Rhyll answered. "As well as supports for the bells."

"I'm guessing insurance?" Nala offered. "I dare say if they replaced any floors, they'd need stairs, then every tourist would want to climb it. An insurance nightmare, I've no doubt. Probably better for all this way."

It started to sprinkle as the trio trekked back down the hill to the car and drove around to see what accommodation was available.

"It might be weird, but staying at a B&B seems too personal — like invading someone's private home. A hotel, on the other hand, is preferable."

"How about this one then?" Dan asked, stopping in the street in front of a row of shops.

"Where?" Nala craned her head out the window.

Dan pointed. "There's the sign. I think we go in through this arcade and the entrance is either at the back or upstairs."

"That yellow building? The Owl? Seems fine enough." Rhyll was about to hop out of the car, but Dan reversed a few metres and then mounted the curb to drive into the arcade. "Just getting the car out of the rain and undercover before that drone circles back." There was barely enough room to open the doors.

"Paranoid much?" Nala joked.

"Being prudent, again." Dan squeezed out of the car, following the others with their packs. "I'd prefer to be playing it safe."

Once they were inside and rooms found, they sat in the lounge and watched the news, mainly following the steady progress of the death wave. Some broadcasters understandably spent more time on the dilemmas in their locality, so a bit of channel surfing was required to get news from other affected areas like America, Egypt, and Brazil.

While the terrain, languages and cultures were vastly different, the sight of panicked families fleeing for their lives was the same around the globe.

"Getting to Mount Kailash is going to be tricky," Dan

considered. "I think the nearest airport is Kathmandu. After that, it's road or trail over the Himalayas."

"How about hoverpods?"

"In theory they'd be ideal, but it would cost a mint to pay someone to risk it. Getting there by land will be a long and arduous trip."

"If there's a silver lining to the death wave, it's that there's not going to be anyone to stop us."

"I dunno. Satellite tracking, AI missile systems don't need live people to function ... Who's to say what they've set up to keep people out? It's not as if they've ever been friendly to unwanted incursion."

Rhyll frowned, unhappy with the choices. "Let's worry about that when it happens. Perhaps the Chinese will see the benefit of allowing access."

"Only if they come out best," Dan said cynically.

"Not much has changed during my sleep?" Rhyll muttered.

"With them? No."

"Then they better take note of your interview," Rhyll stated.

While the newscast played out, they searched the kitchen and made themselves dinner.

"Time to organise getting to the next chakra point." Rhyll joined them around the table in the dining room.

"Which is where?" Dan asked.

"It depends on what flights are available. We have four to choose from."

"And what about customs? I thought we only had the certificates for the UK," Nala pointed out.

"That's something I'll have to talk about with Mum, maybe get several for all contingencies. Dan, do you know how long it will take to organise express mail?"

"Depending on timing; getting optimum flights, it can be done within a day. There are costly message pods corporations use; they are hypersonic. Very fast, very expensive. São Paulo is a major city so it shouldn't be a problem, but you can probably get it sent electronically, too."

"Can I?"

"Sure." Dan nodded. "You could have a copy and she could send a backup to the customs agents as a reference and proof of authenticity."

"Not just a mediocre journalist, then," Nala teased.

"Mediocre?" he questioned.

"Now Nala, Dan's more than a mediocre journalist—"

"That's right!" Dan protested, nodding.

"You forgot mediocre driver and mediocre survival forager." Rhyll winked.

"How remiss of me." Nala chuckled.

Dan looked from one to the other. "You can't fool me. I know you treasure every word and bit of advice I give."

After a late breakfast they packed food and a thermos of coffee for the road and made their way out of town for the drive back to London. They paused on the road so Dan could get another picture of the tor and the lone bell tower.

"He takes his pictures seriously, doesn't he?" Rhyll said softly to Nala while he was out of the car.

"At least he takes something seriously."

The driving was uneventful, not surprising considering these sections of the adjoining shires had been evacuated. There was the opportunity to revisit Stonehenge and the ongoing festivities, but Rhyll declined. They watched the festival fires and gathering as they passed.

"We'd be there for hours," she said. "And like I said yesterday, I'm not one for crowds."

"Maybe Dan needs another plate of food?"

"On second thoughts, we've lives to save." Dan accelerated.

They were now on the M3, passing Basingstoke, where they came across a roadblock. Vehicles had been parked across all the lanes to ensure no thoroughfare except where the police vehicles waited.

"I wonder if they're remotely controlling this blockage," Dan said, spying more street-cams near the overpass. "There's cameras everywhere."

"But why block the exit route? You'd think they'd be wanting to stop people entering," Nala said. The other section of the motorway wasn't manned at all.

Four figures in police issue EV suits stood by the vehicles, watching the Range Rover approach.

"That answers that question." Dan slowed. "No droids."

"Looks like they were expecting us." Rhyll shook her head. "Haven't they learnt yet that EV suits won't help them?"

The officers paired off, two each side of the road. One waved them to stop.

"G'day, officers." Dan wound down the window, but the officers waved them out at gun-point.

"Sir. Turn the vehicle off. All occupants are to get out."

"Anyone fancy their chances?" Dan muttered, engine still running.

"I'd rather not, and they could be here because of the interview. We know if we get arrested again it won't be for long," she said sadly.

"At gunpoint?" Dan turned the motor off and opened his door, showing his empty hands. Nala and Rhyll did the same, following the instructions to move to the front of the car. The officers moved closer and promptly sprayed something into the trio's faces.

Nala, Dan and Rhyll collapsed to the ground.

CHAPTER NINE

RHYLL OPENED HER EYES, SQUINTING AT THE GLARE OF THE SUN. Judging from its new angle, several hours had passed. When she used the headrest of the front seat to pull herself upright, she sensed Nala was gone before she saw it. Dan was missing, too.

Through the windscreen, the road ahead showed no signs of life, just the vehicles straddling the lanes as before. No police were visible.

"Assuming they were police," she muttered. Rhyll climbed out of the car to clear her head, get the blood flowing and exercise cramped muscles.

A stiff breeze came down from the northeast. Through the trees she could see fields and cows, the rooftops of a distant village.

The buzzing of the two remaining drones could be heard circling above. As she looked up, her phone rang. The number was hidden, but only a few friends knew her number anyway, and she was sure it wasn't her mum or Cataleya calling.

"Miss Ellis. We need to talk," she heard the unfamiliar voice say.

"Where are my friends? Who are you and what have you done with them?"

"Not to worry. Your friends are in a safe place for now."

"How? This is a dead zone; no one capable of entering and leaving would defy me to do your bidding."

"Defy you? Those are strange words coming from a young girl. Illusions of grandeur, perhaps?"

"Why not meet me in person and find out for yourself!"

"Ah, there's the feisty spirit. That's what I wanted to see—"

"You really don't want to see me feisty, and you haven't answered my questions. Who and how?"

"You can't guess? You haven't met *me* yet, only my incompetent accomplices. Maybe one day ... As to the 'how', it's easy to find desperate volunteers if you know where to look. They knew they would probably die doing this if they took too long, but guarantees were made that their families would be safe for the rest of their lives if they were successful. Like you, I'm willing to make sacrifices for the bigger picture."

It seemed obvious it was Tyrone Stradjek. "If anything happens to Dan or Nala, I'll do everything in my power to find you."

"Aren't you on a schedule to save the world? Are your two friends worth more than the millions of lives you say you can save?"

"What do you want?"

"I have your diamonds. And I'm happy to let you have them back."

"That's great; otherwise everyone will die, including you."

"Exactly why we're talking. Please explain to me what it is that's happening. I'm curious."

"Have you been under a rock these last weeks? I'm probably wasting my breath."

"You're going to insist the earth is killing us?"

"Isn't it? You tell me what's happening, then. Please explain how there's a 100% mortality rate in the affected areas. Tell me how none of the best pandemic agencies can begin to understand; why they're losing their most experienced people."

"Obviously, I can't—"

"Exactly. Yet you refuse to believe the one and only explanation that fits all criteria."

"That the earth is killing us?" Although she couldn't see his face, he sounded incredulous.

"Defending itself against an out-of-control infection, like any living entity will do if it's capable."

"But the Earth isn't living—"

"The evidence to the contrary is all around you. I'm obviously talking to an idiot. You just have to open your mind and eyes—"

"Enough! If you want the diamonds back, you will go to Niger in Africa. I've sent one of the diamonds to Niels Franke."

"Who's he?"

"Competition. Once you finish him off, you can pry the diamond from his dead hands and continue your work."

"Oh, so *now* you believe something inexplicable is happening? But instead of trying to understand how or why, you just want to use it for your own greed and power grab!"

"Exactly. I'm relieved that wasn't too difficult for you to grasp."

"What about the other diamonds?"

"I'll present one at a time after I'm satisfied you've accomplished your task."

"You realise this is pointless? Unless you adapt, you will die, and if I fail, everyone will die anyway."

"Let's say I'm counting on you not having a death wish, and I have alternate plans for my continued good health and survival. Your concern is retrieving the diamonds. I'll even make it easy for you since you're doing me a favour. I've left you a voice-activated AI hoverpod, so no more hire cars; no more hassles through customs and security. The pod has the coordinates you need and I'll be tracking you every step. Oh, and one last thing. If your friends aren't enough to ensure your swift action, I can get to your mother whenever I want."

The phone went dead.

When Rhyll looked behind the Range Rover, she saw the

hoverpod about thirty metres back, parked diagonally across the lanes. She spent a few minutes wondering what to do next — go and do Tyrone's bidding or try to find her friends? As the wind shifted, so did the sound of the drones. She looked up.

"Who are you guys?" She had an idea. Searching through the glovebox was fruitless, unless she wanted to know about upcoming auctions in Amesbury.

Rhyll walked to the remaining police vehicle, finding two officers slumped inside; both had been shot at close range. She reached in to pop the boot and rummaged through the contents. Her idea of finding road marking paint proved successful. Taking the can out, she shook it vigorously before spraying the fluorescent yellow paint on the black bitumen. Once completed, she walked back to the Rover to wait by her phone.

After a couple of minutes, it rang.

"Would this be Rhyllien Ellis?" It was a male, English voice.

"I'm sure you know it is. Who are you?" She looked up as one of the drones lowered slightly, facing directly at her.

"I'm Brody Thurston. We've met."

"The reporter from the other night? I had a suspicion it was you. Did your drone record any of this?"

"As it so happens we did witness the kidnapping. Four figures drove north."

"You didn't track them?"

"You're the hot item for the moment. Our other drones are busy with the troubles elsewhere so we couldn't cover both. Nevertheless, CCTV along the roads will pick them up. Once they move out of the quarantine zone, I'm sure the authorities will apprehend them."

"Have you reported the kidnapping to the police? They killed the officers here."

"We've reported it, but that area is now cut off and they're run off their feet with the evacuations. However, I dare say the street cameras will have recorded it all as well. These men will definitely be apprehended."

Rhyll looked around, eventually seeing the camera high up the pole.

"Why were your friends kidnapped, but not you?" Brody continued.

"What do you know about me, Mr Thurston?"

Brody recited the usual stuff; nothing too in-depth and nothing new. "Though I do find it incredible you're here. And still alive."

"*Impossible* more like it. Want a DNA sample?"

"No need. Considering what I've seen, I'll take you at your word."

"I'm told you've been following the story online."

"It's a smashing bit of news. Your friend — Daniel, is it? He's done an exceptional job in getting the word out about you."

"I wasn't sure if it was the right thing to do—"

"You're someone to be reckoned with now."

"Yet here I am; Tyrone Stradjek has just reckoned with me."

"Tyrone Stradjek?"

"He's behind this. What can you tell me about him?"

"Hmm. Not a great deal. His grandfather founded the Volaris Corporation. Heavily into arts and antiquities—"

"I killed his father. That is why he's doing this."

"Doing what, exactly? And how and when did you kill his father?"

Rhyll told him about the robbery when her own father was murdered, in greater detail than had ever been made public. "As to what I have to do ... One last question: What can you tell me about Niels Franke?"

"Niels Franke? I should get Johnson, he's the finance and resources guru. Umm ..." There was a long pause. "Franke's an eco-mining magnate in Africa, but more recently he's been delving seriously into asteroid mining. That's where the big movers are looking at the moment. Expensive set up initially, but the projected revenue over the long-run looks promising. Why?"

"Tyrone Stradjek wants me to kill him."

"Kill Franke? You? You're not an attack hoverpod."

"I know, I'm just a kid. Hard to believe."

"How are you supposed to do it?" Brody asked.

"I'll make it look like an accident. How ... I'll work on that."

"Johnson's just mentioned Stradjek's recently been dipping his toes into off-world mining too."

"That explains the 'why'. I guess he wants to remove competition. He — or Volaris — was involved in the Erdany mining group in Brazil."

"Johnson agrees." The drone pivoted. "I see he left you a hoverpod. I was wondering about that. It arrived half an hour ago."

"His way of making things easier for me, therefore for *him*."

"You don't want to be there for your friends?"

"They were kidnapped to keep me in line. If I don't at least look like I'm doing as told, it could complicate things further."

"Complicate things further? I suspect you're not telling me all there is to know."

"My mother's in danger too, but she's in Brazil. Just something else I need to deal with; something else he'll have to answer for."

"I see. Shall we meet to arrange things?"

"Not going to happen. Tyrone's got the hoverpod tracked. Any undue delay or diversion will seem suspect, and I'm not putting my friends at risk." She wandered across to the hoverpod as she spoke.

"How are we to get the scoop otherwise?"

"I don't know." Rhyll considered, watching the drones overhead. "Who owns the other drone?"

"That's DIC, going by the logo on the side."

"Will your drone fit through this doorway? It's about seventy centimetres wide."

"I believe it will," he said, after the drone had lowered to a couple of metres.

"Then that's how. I'll take it with me. You can launch it when I arrive in Niger and video whatever happens."

"We can arrange global observation and control through our affiliated agencies. Are you really going to kill Franke?"

"Tyrone has given him something I need. Without it, everyone dies. Since I'm flying international and in the air for hours, I'll need to get some supplies. Please do what you can to help Nala and Dan." She hung up.

Rhyll remembered there was an off-ramp a few hundred metres back along the M3. She turned her attention to the car. Dan made it look easy, but also spoke about the automation of them since she was last a passenger.

Even Nala had knew of it, but not seen it in action.

"I doubt there's much call for it in São Lucas," Dan had said. "No infrastructure."

What Rhyll did recall was the switch to go manual or full-automatic. She selected the latter. Now she had to indicate the address.

"Damn." She spent a few minutes working the GPS, searching for a market. Soon a Tesco's showed up. "Tesco Metro, Basingstoke," she spoke loudly.

The screen blinked for a second before zooming in on the location, with a blue line indicating the route. The screen looked similar to the one in the hoverpod back in Manaus.

"ETA twelve minutes." The engine started and the car started moving. "Obstruction ahead. Rerouting." This took longer, as there was no way of moving forward on the correct side of the road.

The car shifted gear and began driving backwards at speed, steering around the hoverpod on the road until it was able to use the off-ramp as normal. The blue line reappeared, and off she went.

It was one thing being driven by another person, but extremely uncomfortable seeing the steering wheel turn of its own volition. "Better than the alternative."

"Designate alternative route request."

"Umm ... disregard."

With Brody's drone following, the Rover continued as normal, arriving at the large complex on time.

Finding the right trousers with lots of pockets proved frustrating, but eventually she was satisfied. After half an hour, with her trolley of goods, Rhyll sat in the food court to access the Wi-Fi. There was still plenty of fresh food fit to eat so she grabbed fruit and bags of nuts as well. If Nala was with her, she'd say Rhyll had taken survival foraging to a new level.

Although they joked about it, she was now thankful for Dan's paranoia and his tips regarding non-traceability. She made a note of the numbers in her phone — there were only a handful — turned it off, removed the SIM to tape it inside the phone casing, then removed the battery and tossed it all into her pack. Even if the DIC drone saw her number, they couldn't trace her or contact her.

After charging, she placed a couple of burner phones on the table, used the VPN Dan had installed on her tablet to connect to the store's free Wi-Fi, and activated the new SIMs with a temporary email address through a Swiss site he'd put her onto. "They don't log VPN use, so anonymity is better," he had said.

Once the burner phones were activated, she turned off GPS and Bluetooth and, despite the time difference, called her mother to tell her about all the happenings.

"I'll message Nala and Dan as well," she said afterwards. "I'll be circumspect in case the kidnappers have their phones, and then dump this one." Rhyll gave her mother the number for the second burner phone. "That's the number my next message or call will come from."

Her voice messages to Nala and Dan were identical: *"This is Rhyll. Stradjek is using me as a tool to wipe out his competition; my first visit is somewhere in Niger and you're leverage to keep me in line. If you hear this message, stay safe. And to the kidnappers if you are hearing this, you are fools to believe Stradjek will keep his word."*

To Cataleya she recorded. *"Hi Cat. This is Rhyll. Having a fun time here in the UK. Big favour, any chance you guys can keep an eye on my mother? Call her at least? Long story. Chat soon."* Rhyll dismantled the phone and tossed it in the electronics recycle bin before returning to the car to load her supplies. As she drove back to the hoverpod, a light rain began to fall.

Tyrone's pod was a luxurious two-seater personal flyer unlike the previous pods in Brazil, which had minimal comfort and amenities. According to the Nav the estimated flight to the Niger coordinates would be almost nine hours. Rhyll was glad this one had a small cubicle in the back for ablutions.

When Brody's drone landed, it took a bit of manoeuvring to get it through the entrance, but eventually she put it inside the pod. She then transferred her gear from the back of the Rover.

Rhyll went through all her gear to see what was missing, but surprisingly only the diamonds were gone. At first she thought it was good of Stradjek to only take the diamonds; then she considered his actions so far, deciding it was more likely incompetence than goodwill. After the DIC incident she had decided to keep everything separate; only the diamonds had been in her pockets.

She settled into her seat and put her harness on. There was a note on the console: "Push me." With nothing left to lose, she did so.

The console lit up, the engine vibrated gently to life, and the door hissed closed. A minute later the hoverpod rose sedately and turned to the southeast.

A blue line on the navigation screen indicated the route, a blinking dot showing the craft's current location.

It was soon dark outside and there was little to see other than the dim lights of the towns twenty thousand metres below. She snacked on her foraged fruit and nuts while reading items of news from the console display.

Having the pod was a boon, but not if it was wasted in

kowtowing to Stradjek's whims; she worried about the amount of time it would take to traverse the globe, and the growing death toll.

When Rhyll first awoke in the cavern in Brazil, it had surprised her how little empathy she had, certain she wasn't like that before her transformation. She was still the fun-loving, outgoing rambunctious teenager, but there was more; a deep well of fury and antipathy that had rarely bubbled to the surface. But it was there, and its potential scared her, even more after her time in the barrow.

She had little control of it if she was angry or stressed in any way; the first time at the Erdany mine was ignorance, but what happened in Winchester was all on her. Could she so easily brush off the fact that she'd instigated the beating, knowing the fury and antipathy would rise causing hundreds of deaths?

But many more would have died if I was incarcerated longer.

Rhyll dozed on and off, a mixture of dreams and troubling visions clouding her sleep.

The beeping console woke her. It was night, the clear sky full of stars.

"Programmed coordinates reached. Landing approach approved. Commencing descent." The message flashed on-screen.

The pod was now above a flat and barren moonlit terrain. Expanding the screen showed she was near the southwestern border of Niger, with Burkina Faso to the south.

"What's the local time?" she asked as she looked out through the wrap-around window.

"01:13"

"Well, that's shit." Her next task was to deal with the drone. "Open door."

"Unable to comply. Safety protocol breach."

Rhyll could use the manual release, but being so close to the door when it burst open was a concern. She saw the *In Case of Emergency* label to the side of the console.

"I authorise override 'Alpha Sierra 3-4 X-ray'. Open the damn door, this is an emergency!"

"Emergency override engaged. Stand clear." A light flashed red above the door as the seal released with a loud hiss. Lucky nothing was loose within the cabin, as the sudden negative pressure would have sucked it out.

Once the turbulence subsided, Rhyll lifted Brody's drone and carried it to the exit, wary of the gusts of air trying to suck her out. She turned it to face outwards, then pressed the 'activate' button and waited for the start-up procedure to complete. When all the relevant lights lit up, she pushed it to the door.

Moments later, whoever was activating it from the other end took control; the drone lifted off the floor and immediately disappeared into the darkness.

"That's my end of the bargain done. It's all yours now, Brody," she muttered.

With four minutes to go before landing, Rhyll had to calm herself, trusting the AI to land safely on the barely lit pad below. She sat in the chair, closed her eyes and tried to relax as much as she could. Even when the pod gracefully set-down and the fresh night air and dust wafted through the open door, she remained still, only opening her eyes when she heard voices.

The console beeped, flashing: *Incoming communication.*

Rhyll put the headset on.

"I see you've landed. Remember, if I don't hear of this death wave soon, I can't guarantee the safety of your friends. Don't fail them. See that green button on the top right-hand side of the console?"

"Yes."

"When you're ready for take-off, hit that and I'll be in touch shortly after. It had better be good news."

Before she could respond, the line went dead. She had been in the air for nine hours; either Nala and Dan were still captives, or he hadn't heard of their release. *Assuming they had been released.*

"Bastard." Rhyll flung the headphones off and stomped her

foot. She heard a crack underneath where her foot connected with a panel.

Outside she could see a line of soldiers, and she realised with the pod's interior lights off, they couldn't see in.

On a whim, and still feeling unsure about the upcoming encounter, she got up and quickly grabbed the most important items from her pack: the tablet, notebook, prism and disc. Rhyll looked around the interior. *Where to hide this damn stuff.*

The storage cupboard was obviously the first place they'd look; the ablutions cubicle was basically a modular, seamless wall. Most of the cockpit was moulded and padded. She knelt on the floor and slid into the footwell underneath the console.

The panel that had taken the brunt of her tantrum was now loose.

Excellent. Perhaps I should throw a tantrum more often.

She pushed the items through, and they slid to the floor with a soft clunk. *At least they're out of sight.* She then tried to pull the damaged section back into place, but the crack was still visible. *Let's hope they don't look too hard.*

Rhyll stood, brushed at her clothes and hair before walking to the exit and the awaiting group.

CHAPTER TEN

IT WAS A BARE ROOM: NO CARPET, NO WALL COVERINGS, BUT telltale *clean* areas where pictures had hung. She could see the shadow of the bars on the one dirty, frosted window. The floorboards were rough and the heads of many tacks indicated carpet had been laid previously.

Nala quickly realised she was alone and her hands were zip-tied in front. She wiped her eyes and awkwardly stood propped against the wall, the effect of the sleep gas she had inhaled slow to wear off. The window frame had been painted over many times, so there was no chance of opening it. Smashing it was an obvious option.

At the door she listened, but there were no other sounds and she wondered where Daniel and Rhyllien were. Twisting the loose doorknob proved the wooden door was locked.

Try as she might, there were no memories since the initial kidnapping; the last thing she saw was the guy in an EV suit spray something in her face. She had no idea where she was or what time it was, though her bladder was saying it had been several hours.

Nala banged on the door. "Hello? Assholes? Anyone there?"

She kicked the door several times, but no one came to investigate. *Puta!*

Kicking the door one final time, she moved to the window, thinking that smashing glass might provoke a response. The room was devoid of any furnishings. Nala took off a boot, shielded her eyes and struck one of the four panes firmly with the heel. The noise seemed loud in the silence. She kept tapping until the glass was knocked out. Still no one came to investigate.

Looking through the gap revealed an abandoned industrial estate. There was a large river and a railway beyond the wire fence. The uniform opalescence of the overcast sky removed any chance of judging the directions, but it was late afternoon.

With utmost care Nala awkwardly sawed her zip-tie along the edge of a shard within the frame, held firm by fifty-year-old putty. Despite a few minor scratches, her hands were free.

The bars were rusty, but only superficially, and the solid brickwork wasn't about to let the bars go. Her room appeared to be about five metres above a large roof. From the little she could discern of the building, it seemed she was in part of an old warehouse complex.

"That's a leg breaker," she muttered, looking down at the drop. After replacing her boot, Nala went back to the door and kicked it a few more times.

"Nala?" she heard. It sounded like Dan. "Is that you?"

"Dan!" From the loudness of his voice, she guessed he was in the next room to her left, and she stepped closer and knocked on the wall to confirm.

"The one and only," Dan called, knocking in reply.

Nala discovered the internal walls weren't brick and mortar. She turned her back to it, and using the sole and heel, began kicking it as hard as she could. Many kicks later, she felt the thick plasterboard give a little. She could hear Dan kicking from the other side. Sweating with the effort, they eventually made a hole large enough to see each other, though they had to kneel to do so.

She saw Dan's wrists were also tied. Nala fetched a shard of glass. "Slip your hands through. I'll cut the zip-ties."

"Don't cut yourself," Dan said as he stretched his arms through the gap.

Nala carefully sawed until the ties were cut.

"Thanks," he said, rubbing his wrists. "Know where we are? I was hoping Rhyll was with you."

"I've no idea where we are, or where she is. I've been kicking and yelling, but there's no response from anyone."

"Perhaps she still unconscious in another room?" Dan suggested.

"Sounds like a good reason to get out, but I suspect she'd be saving us if that was the case."

"And no one has come to investigate the noise. That's weird," Dan said.

"Either we've been left alone for a while — can't think why — or something's happened to them, whoever they are."

"Not cops, then?"

"I very much doubt it. If they were, why here and not the police station? My room's pretty dark with only a small window, high up. What about yours?"

"A window, yes, but it's barred and about two floors above a warehouse roof." Nala then described the view from her window.

"Two floors doesn't seem too bad. If you're dangling, your feet are—"

"And the bars? They're solid. Is there anything of use in your room?"

"Only a length of timber. Nothing that would break down doors or bars."

Nala considered the options. "Might be useful to ram a larger hole."

"Okay. I'll see what I can do. Better stand back."

Nala heard Dan's grunt as he stood up. As she got up off the floor, her bladder insisted on attention. "The assholes could've left a damn bucket!"

"What was that?" Dan asked.

"Nothing."

The banging started shortly after.

After her nature call, she decided to smash more windows to see if all the bars were solid. They were.

A quarter of an hour later the hole in the partition wall was large enough. A sweaty Dan wriggled between the wall's structural timbers and joined Nala with a brief hug.

"You okay?" he asked.

"I'll be better once we're out of here, but thanks." She moved back to the window.

Dan joined her and they studied the distant local environs for a few minutes, but other than some swans by the river and the sound of aircraft high overhead, there was no sign of local human activity.

"That could be the Thames," he said. "I recall it was much further north of the motorway and Basingstoke, but I've no idea what city this is."

"I've not seen any traffic on those roads either."

"So we're still in the cordoned off area. Perhaps our kidnappers left it too late and are dead?" he suggested.

"That doesn't bode well for us then."

"Then we'll just have to get ourselves out." He tried the bars, but they wouldn't budge. He turned, wondering if the two of them could work to get out the small window in his room. He walked to the hole, sticking his head through. He paused and stepped back.

"Actually, we've both been a bit obtuse." He reached for the beam of wood he'd used to batter the wall. "It's obvious these rooms weren't designed to hold prisoners." He started ramming the wall beside the door. It, too, was a cavity wall lined with heavy-duty plasterboard.

"Better watch out for electrical wires," Nala warned.

Dan grunted in response. When a fair-sized hole was made,

they both grabbed the edges and heaved, pulling the board from the framework in a shower of dust and old insulation.

"See? Not just a pretty face." Dan smiled, pleased with himself.

"I was going to say a lucky guess, but that's a fair comment." She patted his sweaty cheek, leaving a dusty handprint. "Want me to go first?"

He shook his head. "I'd never hear the end of it if you did." He enlarged the hole with a few extra kicks, then stepped through. "There's a long corridor and stairs. It's clear, though it smells of vomit."

The upper half of the opposite wall of the corridor was all louvre windows; some were open, some closed; all most filthy and covered in dust and bird droppings. Through the gaps they could see below the interior of the warehouse: odd bits of machinery, crates, stacks of tyres and drums on pallets.

Dan helped Nala through and together they made their way along the dim corridor, calling for Rhyll as they checked each door they came across. There was no response. The other rooms were empty, and in a short time they found themselves at the top of the stairs.

"Perhaps she's downstairs. Maybe still drugged like we were."

"I still can't sense her," Nala said after a pause.

"You have that ability too?"

"To a lesser degree. It started when we first met—"

"Oh yeah. Back in São Lucas. There was that power outage … I thought it was the lightning, but something happened between you two, didn't it? It was never fully explained."

"I was told when I was a baby, the same thing happened, but much reduced because I was a newborn. Ever since we reconnected, I've always felt her presence. When we were kidnapped in Manaus her presence was still there, but much diminished. Now I can't feel her at all."

"Meaning she's a long way away?"

Nala shrugged. "I hope that's the reason."

"What else? Oh—" Dan stopped, not wanting to think of the alternative. He continued to move down the stairs.

The metal structure creaked loudly during the descent but they didn't bother to conceal any noise; it was clear no one was around. Further down the source of the foul odour was found, and the pair sidestepped the mess.

Directly below the rooms used to imprison them was another long wall with louvred windows and a door at each end. Through the dusty glass they could see a larger, open-plan office. It seemed the more promising place to find a hint to explain as to what was going on.

Most of the desks still had paperwork on them. The upended chairs and paper littering the floor indicated a hasty evacuation.

Readings Construction Machinery was written on the top of some of the paperwork.

"Looks like we're in Reading." Dan showed her.

"Is that far from where we were before being kidnapped?"

"I guess about 30 kilometres north."

Nala gasped in delight, seeing a sign for the toilets. "I'll see you in a minute." She increased her pace, leaving Dan to look around the office.

"I found one of them," she called out a few minutes later.

Dan raced over to the toilets to see a pair of legs sticking out from under a cubicle door. Inside the cubicle, a man had collapsed next to a toilet bowl. It was obvious from their previous experiences he'd fallen ill and vomited before succumbing to the death wave.

"You okay?" Dan asked Nala.

"We've seen worse. Still ... it was unexpected."

"Reckon he was one of the kidnappers?"

"We can't be sure, but highly unlikely any workers would be loitering after the evac. And there's no overpowering smell, so he must've died recently."

"One way to find out." Dan started searching the body. He found a wallet and went through its contents. "Matthew Smith.

He's from Slough. I'm not sure where that is, but it's not Reading."

"There's nothing to indicate he worked here? No cell phone?"

"Not that I can find. We could try going through the work employment records, but it'd take ages and would be pretty pointless."

"Forget it. Looking for someone to blame, I guess. There were four of them. Maybe finding the others will give us a clue."

They continued their search of the office before moving back into the warehouse area.

At the far end, near a large half-open roller door, they saw another body lying on the concrete floor. He had blotchy skin, but there was also a lot of blood. Closer inspection showed he'd been shot twice in the chest.

"What the hell?" Dan walked closer while Nala continued towards the exit.

He searched the man, avoiding the worst of the blood. He found an empty holster and a damaged phone. It was locked. He bent down and used the man's index finger to unlock it. "Bingo." He quickly went to the settings to ensure the phone wouldn't go to sleep-mode, and was going through the messages when Nala called to him from the large doorway.

"I think I found the shooter."

Outside the warehouse was an open area, part-lorry-turning bay as well as a car park. It had started raining, making the approaching dusk even gloomier. At the compound entrance was a security post and a boom gate. Only a stub of the boom remained, the remainder strewn across the roadway. Thirty metres beyond the gate a police car had mounted the curb, coming to rest against a low brick wall.

The pair jogged through the drizzle to the car and found two more occupants, none in police uniforms. Both were dead; one had died in similar fashion to the one in the toilet, but the driver was covered in pustules, severe rashes, and blood.

Approaching the passenger with distaste, Dan went through

the pockets to check for information. "John Fletcher. This guy's from Dorking. I remember the road signs when we left Gatwick Airport. A long way to commute if he worked here and lived there."

"What about the driver?"

Dan looked at the mess. "I'm not touching him. There's always a John Doe in these mysteries — he can be John Doe."

"There's always a vital clue in the one place no one looked," Nala said.

"You look then."

Nala started walking around. "I thought you were the investigative journalist."

Dan huffed. "Okay, okay. I hate it when you're right."

"Better get used to it." Nala went to the back of the car, quietly chuckling at the noises and grunts Dan was making, glad she didn't have to go through with it herself.

In the back she found a bag of clothing in the boot. A couple of cans of the sleeping agent lay inside. "No sign of our gear. They probably dumped it so it couldn't be tracked."

"Damn. I really liked that camera!"

"Did you lose many photos?"

"No. It all goes directly to the cloud. Just a hassle and expense." He then saw a pistol in the footwell. "Wait." He reached in to retrieve it.

"I wonder why they shot the other guy?"

"Could have been any number of reasons." Dan slipped the gun in his pocket after checking the safety.

"And why were they leaving?"

"Maybe they lost their nerve and panicked after the first one died. They tried to leave and that guy tried to stop them. There was a fight and they shot him with his own gun," Dan conjectured. "There's no holster on these two and no phones. I reckon the other guy was in charge as he had photos of the three of us." He showed her the phone.

The rainfall increased and started to run down the inside of his shirt.

"Who doesn't have a phone with them these days?" he muttered in irritation.

Nala screwed up her face, seeing the unfortunate mess in the driver's seat. "I don't fancy standing in this rain, but I definitely do not want to drive this car."

"That makes two of us. There were a couple of cars back near the warehouse."

"Those houses are closer." Nala pointed to a long row of tenement houses. "Chances are greater of finding keys for a car in someone's home than in a big, empty warehouse."

The pair jogged along the line of houses until they found a car parked in the cracked concrete driveway. The small front yard was unkempt, with weeds everywhere.

"I don't drive Volvos ... and an old rust bucket at that." Dan scowled at the dented and forlorn vehicle.

"It should suit you, considering the way you trashed that Jag."

"Not my fault it wasn't a four-by-four," he argued as they headed for the front door. It was locked. "Besides, I can't drive it."

"Why is that?"

"I haven't got a hat."

"What?"

"It's an unwritten law: one can't drive a Volvo without a hat, preferably a bowling hat," he explained as he searched for something to smash the front window of the house.

"I've never heard of that law before." Nala flipped over the doormat with her boot. "Who would have thought?" she laughed, picking up a key.

The heavy drapes made the interior of the house very dark. There was a large table against a wall, but it was covered in boxes and untidy stacks of papers and magazines. The front room had too much furniture and clutter, it was musty and in dire need of airing. They walked through carefully, but Dan still barked his shins on a coffee table.

"Looks like we found a hoarder," he commented from the

kitchen. He was looking out the back window. The small courtyard was full of junk, with weeds everywhere, and he saw several large rats scurry between the junk piles.

"I bet they only have instant coffee, too." Nala began looking into the cupboards.

"I don't want to sound like a snob ... but with so many empty houses around ... can we please not stay in this ... *dump?*"

"Aww, Dan." Nala pouted. "But this was someone's castle; their pride and joy."

"You seriously think so?" He tried the light switch, but there was no power.

"It's all some people have." She held up a can of instant coffee. "But if you can be a house snob, I'll be a coffee snob. The dust from that warehouse floor would be tastier."

By mutual agreement, they headed back outside and jogged on through the dusk until they found a house and car more to their liking.

"We are terrible people." Nala chuckled ruefully as they jogged down the deserted street. "You know we don't need to stay in someone's home. Like you said the other day, there's plenty of accommodation to be found."

"A hotel? In town?"

"Sure. We'll find a *suitable* car for you and head into the CBD."

"We need to find phones, and I'd like to replace my camera and tablet. It isn't like we're short of choice while there are completely abandoned suburbs and shops."

"Will a Mazda offend your sensibilities?" Nala asked when they found a car in good condition further down the road.

"If I don't fit, you'll have to drive."

CHAPTER ELEVEN

"I believe this is the Broad Street Mall." Nala looked up from the Nav.

"I'll keep an eye out for pedestrians." Dan drove slowly over the herring-bone paving, careful to avoid the many benches, bins and bollards in the dim light. "Look, there's Sainsbury's."

"Is it any good?" Nala asked.

"Good enough for free."

"Since it's a mall, there's a dozen clothes shops to choose from. No need to look for bargains. Survival Foraging-101, grab what you can."

Dan drove the car to the side under the awning and stopped. "And all within easy walking distance to the car park."

"You're hilarious." Nala hopped out and pushed the doors open to a grocery shop.

"I'll get us coffees," Dan called after her as he wandered into the nearest café.

Ten minutes later he was searching for her. Following the noise, he eventually finding her with a trolley of food.

"It feels strange, all these shops lit and open yet completely empty."

Nala nodded in agreement. "They must have left in a hurry.

Thanks." She took the proffered cup. "How thoughtful. A travel mug."

"I try. What's next?"

"Put this in the boot and find some fresh clothes."

It was fully dark when they finally emerged outside, but the mall was now lit with automatic lighting.

"I still feel bad about this." He put a bag of clothing in the back seat.

"You'll get used to it." Nala reached over and pulled the tag off his new jacket.

Shortly after, they found the Penta Hotel just at the western end of the mall. Going by the foyer, it was well-appointed and looked to be a classy place.

"Survival Foraging-102, grab the best suite when you can." Nala went behind the counter and rummaged through the drawers, finding a manager's keycard after several minutes.

Dan found a luggage trolley and collected the gear from the car. Together they used the lift to the top floor, where Nala let him into his suite.

"Wedge your door open if you leave, we've only the one key," she advised, before heading to her suite across the hall and collecting her bags from the trolley.

When he entered his suite, he whistled at the luxury and checked everything out before finding the news channel. A few stations were replaying Rhyll's message. He listened to the reports as he sorted through his bags.

As well as spare clothes, there were a couple of burner phones. Using the inhouse internet, he was going to browse for a local camera or electronics store to get quality gear. Dan found a universal phone charger beside the bed for the damaged kidnapper's phone. He went through the phone and sent everything to one of his burner phones for safe keeping.

"Just in case," he muttered.

There were photos of himself and Nala tied up as part of a

message indicating the success of the mission. Another pic of Rhyll slumped in the back seat of the Rover.

A reply text ordered to take them to the Maidenhead Airport and await further instructions. That had been over eight hours ago, and the number corresponded to a landline that had been called several times.

"Something obviously went sour for them to get stuck in Reading," Dan said to himself. "Or perhaps there was a double-cross."

Using the multiscreen option, Dan searched the web while the news continued on the TV.

A quick browse of the local area gave him the location of a camera store back down the mall. With no closing time, he decided to grab a bite to eat, then head down. Taking Nala's advice, he made sure the door didn't lock behind him before knocking on her door. There was no response, and he realised the faint sound he could hear was the shower.

He quickly scribbled a note and stuck it on his door, then left.

"You got enough gear there?" Nala observed the pile of gadgets on the table when she popped over later that evening. She had her hair tied back and was wearing her new clothes: hiking boots, stretch jeans, long-sleeved sports shirt and a coat.

"Just the essentials." Dan had found an upmarket tablet — a newer version of his old one, same with his camera and smart phone. All the devices were plugged in for charging.

"I got you a replacement, too." He pointed to another smartphone, currently connected to a charger, lying on the coffee table.

"I take it all back. Am I able to retrieve my old number?"

"Sure, it'll take a few minutes to call your provider. As long as you remember all your details. I'll need to do the same. I don't recall any other numbers, though," Dan confessed.

"I know a few. Imogen's and Rhyll's — mine, obviously."

Dan picked up the kidnapper's phone, noting the full charge.

He showed Nala the pictures and messages while double-checking he had taken all he could from it, then pulled the battery and SIM and sealed them in a bag.

"Why did you do that?" Nala asked.

"In case Stradjek is tracking it. I should have done it earlier, but didn't think of it at the time."

"Fair enough." It took over an hour to get Nala's phone transferred, due to phone delays with her provider. Dan was left waiting on hold after getting the runaround.

"Part of the ever-increasing dilemma of the death wave; businesses and call centres will be missing staff, and will be inundated with panicked callers," Nala stated. She was still waiting for the transfer to go through.

Finally, her phone pinged. "It's a voice message from Rhyll!" She put the phone on speaker.

"This is Rhyll. Stradjek is using me as a tool to wipe out his competition; my first visit is somewhere in Niger and you're leverage to keep me in line. If you hear this message, stay safe. And to the kidnappers if you're hearing this, you are fools to believe Stradjek will keep his word."

"It's time-stamped 17:34," Nala noted.

"That's four hours ago. She'll be in transit for several more hours."

"I'll call her back and leave a message to let her know we're safe."

"Try her real number, too. She's using a burner phone, but might still use her old one." Dan turned back to his phone when he heard a voice answer.

Nala moved to her room while Dan lost his temper at his inept provider.

"Hi, Rhyll. Glad to hear you're okay. Dan and I are safe in Reading. The kidnappers died, like all the others. Not sure what we'll do next, or how to get to you, but don't stress about us. Stradjek's a limp dick. Let us know what your plans are when you can, and we'll see what we can do to help from this end."

Irrespective of the time difference, she decided to call Imogen and told her all the news since the last time they spoke.

"I received a message from her a few of hours ago too." Imogen filled her in on the last message from Rhyll, as well as her new number. "So glad you guys are safe. It will be a load off Rhyll's mind. She also said a reporter named Brody Thurston has been helpful. Maybe you should give him a call."

They chatted longer about the conditions over there.

"We only get snippets on these news channels," Nala said.

"The death wave is still spreading from the mine and Manaus, but things seem to have settled a bit around Lake Titicaca. People are still dying, but there are reports of more survivors. I can only guess this crystal Rhyll placed there is working for those that are attuned to it."

"Like in São Lucas, though she was only carrying them around then, and no one knew their power or what to do with them."

"So, the same thing should be happening around Stonehenge and Glastonbury."

"Except everyone's been evacuated." Nala then remembered to tell her about the druids, before finally saying farewell.

"Brody Thurston?" Dan sounded surprised when Nala repeated the gist of the call later.

"She also had some good news: Cataleya and Ileana will be joining her. I think Rhyll contacted them, and they're going to help."

"That sounds good, though I'm surprised at the GHO's generosity."

"Maybe it's not generosity so much, but part of a long-term strategy. They were the first to see what this death wave did, and how some survived. Perhaps they recognise the significance of Imogen's safety, and how it would affect Rhyll's ability to focus on what needs to be done. She lost her dad, and thought she'd lost her mum. The threat of losing her again would be a huge distraction."

"Fair point. I better find Thurston's contact number." Dan did a quick web search and dialled.

"Hello. Brody Thurston speaking."

"Brody. This is Dan Dobson, you may—"

"Hey! Where are you? Did you escape? Have you contacted Rhyll?"

Dan told him all he could about the dead kidnappers, and that they were near some industrial estate in Reading by the river.

"We saw it unfold via the drone. The police were supposed to track their progress via the traffic cams and arrest them once they left the quarantine area. I'll let them know the situation. I'm in the London studios now, but everywhere is havoc. Riots in the street; citizens desperate to leave the country … raining cats and dogs."

"Nowhere will be safe."

"Try telling *them* that."

"We did in that video. Some other stations are still running it. Maybe we need to get more news to the people."

They discussed back and forth how best to do this.

"Send a drone out to Stonehenge. Video the druids, drop them a microphone and interview them," Dan suggested.

"You're the best person to do that; you're in the area and can survive. What about that other good-looking lady? Is she still with you?"

"Nala?"

Nala, hearing her name, popped up her head.

"Yes. Interview her too. Maybe show the masses while druids survive, normal people can survive too. We'll send a drone to you, and record live. Where exactly are you?"

"We're staying at the Penta Hotel in Reading."

"Nice. A drone should be there by morning. Also, I've a file of the recording of the kidnapping. It's only fair I send a link to you."

Dan turned on the tablet and began the setup process for his new device. It felt like it took ages before he could access the link and watch the vid with Nala. Afterwards, he spoke to her about the drone and the idea about returning to Stonehenge, and the suggestion she be interviewed.

"If people aren't convinced by Rhyll's message already, nothing I say will be enough. Let's just revisit the druids and leave it at that."

Nala didn't look comfortable with the idea, so Dan dropped the subject.

"Well, we've had quite a hectic day," she said. "I'm heading to bed. I'll see you for breakfast."

"My shout."

"Such a gentleman." Nala collected her gear. "Thanks again for this."

"It's the least I could do," he said as she waved. "I made a list, and it was at the bottom," he muttered at the closed door.

CHAPTER TWELVE

DESPITE THE HOUR, THE NIGHT AIR WAS WARM AND DRY. BY THE glaring overhead lights, Rhyll saw an array of dark-skinned soldiers with weapons trained on her.

"That's just great. I don't suppose, being a gold mine, they appreciate unannounced visitors in the early hours of the morning." Rhyll stepped out as the last of the dust settled, steeling herself for the expected onslaught of the devastated ground.

"Albarka gareku da kakaninku. Uwar Duniya za ta ƙaunace ku duka," she called out the ritual blessing, since it had helped the previous times. *When did I learn Hausa?* She knew, from traipsing around with her parents, that out of the many dialects of Africa, Hausa was one of the more prominent tongues in these parts.

No one bowed. When the soldiers saw no one else within the pod, they lowered their weapons and relaxed, talking amongst themselves quietly and pointing. Either the blessing had minimal effect, they didn't understand her, or they weren't intimidated by a lone girl.

Their languid response gave Rhyll time to use the remote to close and lock the pod hatch and to fight down the nausea and ire threatening to show itself. She felt as bad here as in Brazil, and clenched her teeth to prevent herself from crying. *Or worse.*

"You are Ms Ellis?" A deep-voiced soldier stepped forward, an officer by the amount of bling on his shoulder.

Rhyll nodded, forcing a smile. "I am." She pocketed the remote.

"Please this way come." He waved politely to the path she was to take.

With two troops in front and two following, she was escorted to a long, low building surrounded by vegetation. The remaining troops marched off back to their barracks.

The low building turned out to be well-appointed guest living quarters of rammed-earth construction.

Leaving the escort in the mosaic-tiled corridor, the young officer opened the door to her suite and showed her around the lounge, kitchenette, bedroom, and a bathroom that was bigger than the hoverpod.

"Please to refresh yourself after your journey. Mr Franke will join you in an hour. I come for you. Can I get you anything for the moment?"

Rhyll shook her head, looking around at the luxurious bungalow, noting the amenities. "I'll be ready when you return."

When he left she heard the door lock. After another walk around her suite, she unpacked the one change of clothes she'd brought. The only other item in her pack was her tablet. When she activated her phone, it pinged twice with messages and missed calls.

"Hi, Rhyll. Glad to hear you're okay. Dan and I are safe in Reading. The kidnappers died, like all the others. Not sure what we'll do next, or how to get to you, but don't stress about us. Stradjek's a limp dick. Let us know what your plans are when you can, and we'll see what we can do to help from this end."

She also received a message from her mum.

"Hello darling. Guess what? I have two of your lovely friends from Manaus here to protect me. Cataleya and Ileana send their love, as do I. Do what you need to do, and don't fret about me. Call me when you can."

The message from her mother had been sent several hours ago, and took a huge load off her shoulders. She was free to follow her gut instincts, regardless of Tyrone's threats, but she wasn't fooled. He had managed to get to them several times before. She wasn't that naïve; he would always be a threat, regardless of what happened here.

Rhyll knew she had to stop him somehow, but didn't have the luxury of time to seek her vengeance; millions of other people could be saved if she was quick enough. Stradjek's fate would have to wait.

She returned the call to her mother, then Nala. It was so exciting to hear their voices, and she told them what she knew so far. "When I know more, I'll tell you, probably before I leave Niger. At least Stradjek is off our backs."

With much relief, she grabbed a quick shower to freshen up for her meeting.

Her escort introduced himself as Michal when he returned. He looked tired but was pleasant as he ushered Rhyll into a large dining room at the end of the long hallway, with no other guards in sight. She was completely taken aback by the enclosed arboretum, and wondered: *Why would you cause so much devastation, only to create such a paradise?* She also now realised the sense of desolation was marginally lessened in here.

There was a water feature on the far side of the dining room. Water cascaded down a textured wall into a pond, then overflowed along an in-ground channel past the tables to create another pond within the garden. A lot of effort had been put into this area to give the ambience of serenity.

Niels Franke was sitting at the large dining table. He looked to be in his mid-forties; he had dark hair and was dressed in jeans, short-sleeved shirt and a khaki vest.

"Ah, Ms Ellis," he said with an Afrikaans accent. When he stood, she estimated his height at about six-foot, slightly taller than her. He offered his hand to shake. When she did, she felt calmness radiating from him; almost like when she was touching Keagan the druid or Cataleya. "Welcome to Niger. Please be seated."

"It's so good of you to see me at such short notice. I guess I should apologise for the lateness of my arrival."

Michal had silently departed, and a waiter now entered. He came forward and pulled her chair out, sliding it back in as she sat, then poured two glasses of mineral water before departing.

"Not at all." Niels sat down after her. "These things happen. It was quite a surprise to receive an express message packet informing me of your imminent arrival, but it gave us time to prepare. I hope you found your suite comfortable."

"It is, and I must say *I'm* quite surprised, considering the time and reasons for my visit. Was that mentioned in the message?"

"It was a cryptic warning of my imminent doom, accompanied with a huge diamond. Who would have done that, do you think? And why?"

"Tyrone Stradjek. He's trying to remove competition for his new space mining venture. He wants you and others like you out of his way."

"So — and no offence — he sends a *teenager* to do his bidding?"

"Surely you've heard of what's happening in Brazil and the Erdany mine?"

"That plague is quite devastating," Niels agreed.

"No plague. Nature's payback ... through me. And he wants a repeat performance here. His aim is to wipe out as much of your enterprise as he can."

"So you're saying this newscast of yours at Stonehenge that includes the message from the shaman ... It's all true?"

"I know it's hard to believe; that's why we did the broadcasts to show people the facts. All you have to do is return the diamond and no one needs to die."

"Yes. I'm curious why anyone would send me a very valuable diamond only to have you come take it away."

"Stradjek believes your greed will prevail and you'll do whatever you can to keep it, thus ensuring a swift death. He hasn't worked out all the details, though."

"Details? Like what?"

"That depends on what your intentions are."

The waiter returned with a tray of entrees and began placing the various plates on the table.

"Please, help yourself," Niels offered as the waiter backed away.

Rhyll nodded, looking at the selection of fruits, nuts and rice dishes.

"You might find the food here different to the typical western diet. We have tuwo shikafa and jollof rice dishes, akara, okpa. The garri can be eaten with these soups." He explained, pointing to the colourful array.

"I can assure you, the western diet is not for me. I'll have fresh, locally produced food any day ... or night." She was hungry after her long journey as her *snacks* didn't quite do the trick, and she needed to restore her energy. "What do you know about Stradjek?"

"Not much. We hear things at certain levels. Millionaires are like a club — everyone knows something about the others, even if they move in different circles and have very little to do with one another." Niels told her a few things about Stradjek's activities — most of which she knew from her mother and the news. "Do you know what we are doing here?" He made his selection after Rhyll.

She tried to remain calm as she spoke. "Aren't you mining — raping and pillaging earth's resources, that sort of thing?"

"We *are* both involved with mines, but where Stradjek and those like him start them, I help fix them. This used to be the largest gold mine in Africa."

"I don't care. It's an abomination; a scar on the landscape, and it has to stop!" Rhyll took a breath.

"I agree."

"You what?" Rhyll stopped, food halfway to her mouth.

132

"We're here to rehabilitate the land the mining has destroyed. I gather you're unaware we only purchased it five years ago? My predecessors mined it dry and sold it quite cheaply. A small part of my company sifts through the tailings in the chance of recovering enough to cover our costs, using enhanced and refined techniques — too much trouble with little to gain for its predecessors — but every credit we raise goes back into rehabilitating the landscape, which is a very slow process — there being so much devastation. We use permaculture techniques where we can; however, due to the degradation of the soil, we need to bring in external resources. It's time-consuming, so there may not be much to see for our efforts. I can understand if you thought the mine was still operational. Eventually we will reintroduce the native flora and fauna."

"I had no idea." Rhyll was flummoxed. "Then why would he send me here?"

"As you say, to remove competition so he can have free reign in his next venture. However, I don't think Stradjek has much of an idea about my real work; in an effort to minimise the destruction of the Earth, my company has diverted much of its capital into off-world mining. Off-world mining will be extremely beneficial to Earth, not to mention lucrative to those who can get a foothold in it first. I suspect that's why he regards me as competition, and was all that was needed to get on his bad side. I should also point out that a substantial amount of any off-world profits will be going into the rehabilitation of old mines."

Rhyll chewed in silent contemplation.

Later, after the plates were cleared, Niels went on in detail about the surveying of the pit walls and the plans to make it into a lake and wetland area, as well as his intention to bring in soil to begin the native revegetation program.

"While in many respects all effort should be to bring it back to its original condition, it's been so long and the area is so degraded, we're doing the next best thing. It would be a shame if we all died trying to do that. Perhaps later we can go on a tour, to show you our work."

"That would be great, but I really need to get moving as soon as possible."

"Understandable. I just thought you should know there are others who find this open-cut mining appalling."

Rhyll couldn't release the death wave here; his words and her instincts — what she sensed from him — told her that. Even though her friends were safe, she wondered how she could fool Tyrone; make him believe she'd followed his instructions. *He may not yet be aware of his men's fate.*

"What else can you do with your powers?" he asked.

Rhyll nearly choked on her food. "My *powers?*"

"The shaman gave the impression that the power of Mother Nature flowed through you."

"Well ... I wouldn't go as far as that."

"Yet you can create a ... What are they calling it on the news?"

"Death wave?"

"That's it. You have this ability to cause a death wave — the wrath of Gaia — and you don't think it's a form of power? Have you been able to do other things we mere mortals can't? The newscast shows you boldly rendering first-aid on a lion. Can you talk to animals?"

The memory of summoning the piranha came to mind. "Not *talk* as such, but I can sense their feelings and can calm them—"

"You do realise that's not normal? If you can create a death wave, can you create a 'life wave' too?"

"Life wave?"

"Reverse of a death wave." Niels grinned. "Nature doesn't just kill; she creates and heals, too."

Rhyll put her fork down. "I *have* healed people, just never thought of it that way — using it to heal the land. I thought that's what the diamonds were for."

"There you go. Maybe you should try it."

"I wouldn't know how."

"Did you know how to create the death wave?"

"Not at first — that was an accident — I didn't know it was me."

"But you learnt?"

"Yes ... When I'm in danger or stressed-out, I can make it happen."

"Maybe when you're completely at ease, it will come to you. Have you ever meditated before, or done yoga?"

"A bit." Rhyll considered this new train of thought. "Assuming it works, but that doesn't help my situation; I want to keep Stradjek believing he's got me under his thumb. As long as he believes that, my friends will remain safe."

"How is Stradjek going to find out what happened?"

"I guess he'd hear it on the news. There's a UKTV news drone recording what transpires here." Rhyll informed Niels of her arrangement with Brody.

"That would work, but also make things awkward. What would indicate your success?"

"He'll be expecting to hear all your activity and communications have ceased. Maybe a few bodies."

"I can work out those details. What sort of time limitations are we looking at?"

Rhyll thought back to the previous death wave occurrences. "If I activated it immediately, then there'd be sickness within hours and deaths soon after."

"So soon? That's appallingly impressive."

"The last thing he said was if he didn't hear anything within twenty-four hours, my friends would pay for it," Rhyll added.

"We can't have that."

She decided not to reveal to Niels her friends weren't in so much danger now. "Finally, assuming I was successful, he'd see the hoverpod activate and move to the next chakra location. He knows I wouldn't leave here without the diamond."

"Chakra location?"

Rhyll told him about the Earth chakras and the effects she believed they had in the saving of lives for those attuned to Earth.

"Puts a whole new meaning to the term 'living in harmony'."

Niels reached into his pocket. "And to show *my* integrity ..." He handed her the blue diamond.

"I don't know what to say." *Maybe that was the* calmness *I felt entering the room earlier?* She reached for it, feeling its warmth and soothing vibration immediately. This man, almost a complete stranger, simply held out over eight hundred thousand credits of gemstone.

"Say nothing. I can bring more food if you wish. I'll begin organising the procedure to halt communications and activity."

"This has been great, and very enlightening. If you don't mind, I better get some rest before I try anything. In the past, *healing* has been very taxing." They bid each other farewell.

Back in her suite, Rhyll activated a burner phone, deciding to make some calls despite the time differences.

CHAPTER THIRTEEN

Dan woke to the sound of a drone hovering outside. He threw a robe on and staggered to his balcony. It was daylight, though overcast with a cold breeze. When he spotted the drone, he waited until it saw him. He gave it a thumbs-up, pointed to his watch and indicated *one*, and went back inside hoping they worked out *one hour*.

He heard Nala in the kitchen. "I was going to do that," he said when he wandered into the other room.

"If I waited any longer, it'd be lunch."

"Good morning to you too. I didn't know we were on a schedule. The drone's here, by the way. We can go as soon as we're ready."

"Rhyll called earlier this morning." Nala repeated the gist of the call. "She'll let us know where she's headed when she leaves Niger."

"Good news."

Forty minutes later, with a thermos of hot coffee for the road, they began the return trip to Somerset, driving through the town centre to get to the M4 with the drone following several hundred metres overhead.

"There's someone else ahead!" Dan pointed, slowing the car.

As they were leaving Reading, they saw two vehicles: a dark red van and an old dilapidated Landcruiser driving up the road. "Maybe we can include some new faces in the interview," Dan suggested.

"Perhaps they're part of the kidnap crew?" Nala sounded dubious. "Or more fools conned by Stradjek?"

He slowed down. "Good points. Let's see what they're up to."

The van stopped by the curb ahead while the four-wheel drive accelerated, smashing through the front windows of a building.

Glass shattered, showering the vehicle, and the aluminium framework of the windows buckled and fell across the car's roof.

"What the fuck!" Dan said in surprise.

He drove closer, then realised the building was a bank. Five people hopped out of the van — two from the front and three from the rear. They carried empty bags towards the building, where they joined the limping driver of the now-smoking Landcruiser. Alarms were ringing loudly.

"It's a bank robbery!" Dan exclaimed. He quickly grabbed his camera, starting to take snapshots.

"Looks like it. Put the bloody camera away and let's go!"

Dan dropped the camera into his lap and turned down the nearest side street, hoping they weren't noticed. "You reckon they'll survive long enough to spend any of it?"

"Wrong mentality I suspect, so that would be a 'no'. You've seen how quickly they succumb. I doubt they'll get beyond the death zone limits."

Following the GPS, the pair left the CBD area quickly and sped west.

"There goes another traffic camera." Dan spotted the flash as he sped through another intersection. He had gradually gotten over his nervousness about driving through red lights. Now he barely gave it a glance.

"Four things; I doubt anyone is manning the monitor, I doubt anyone will send the ticket, and I doubt anyone will be paying. And this isn't your car."

"Still, it still feels weird."

"All this is weird. Everywhere is a ghost town, but everything is still functioning." Nala watched as they left the suburbs and the green fields became more prevalent. "I miss Brazil," she mused.

"You know," Dan considered as he negotiated a large roundabout to follow the M4. "We're probably safer staying within this death wave zone, away from Stradjek and his henchmen."

"At least until we hear from Rhyll. I hope we can work something out by then." She was checking her phone for messages when the back window of their car shattered.

"Shit." Dan swerved out of surprise, but recovered quickly.

"What the fuck was that?" Nala jumped with fright and dropped the phone.

"Did I hear gunshots?"

Dan glanced in the mirror, recognising the red van. "Those bank robbers are behind us!" The Mazda raced forward as he planted his foot.

Nala twisted in her seat to look back. She could barely see into the dark interior of the red van, but saw an elbow protruding from the passenger window. "I can only make out two figures. The driver and the shooter. How'd they sneak up on us?"

"We're the only people in a fifty-kilometre radius. I didn't think I needed to keep checking my mirrors."

"Well, someone's here now!"

"I assume they think we were witnesses."

"We were, and you took bloody pictures." Nala looked long and hard to see if there were more in the van, or perhaps a second car further back.

They ducked as more gunfire was heard, but the shots went wide.

"Where's that gun you grabbed from the warehouse?" she asked.

"In the bag — back seat."

Nala reached down the side for the seat lever, pushed back to make her chair recline and quickly opened the bag, feeling for the gun.

"You know how to handle it?" he asked.

"I won't shoot you if that's what you mean. You forget, all Brazilians do a year's national service."

"Shoot their tyres," Dan suggested.

"That's not going to happen, especially from this angle with only a handgun ... even if I leant out the side like in the movies."

"You can do that?"

Nala ignored him as she checked the weapon and the magazine. "It's a Glock Gen 12.9 millimetre—"

"You remember all that from your one year national service years ago?"

"No, it's written on the barrel." She removed the clip to check the ammunition. "It's got a fifteen-round mag with ... thirteen rounds left." Keeping low, Nala rolled awkwardly onto her stomach in her seat and took aim at the pursuing van. "Keep the car steady." Using the headrest as support for her wrist, she fired an answering volley.

Her shots cracked their windscreen. The van swerved and slewed sideways into the guard rail of the centre strip of the motorway.

"Good shooting," Dan complimented as he sped away.

"We were lucky. I think only one of my shots hit."

"Lucky or not, it worked." Dan checked the mirror without slowing. The other car was much further back, but still following.

"I don't think they expected to be fired upon." Nala resumed her sitting position, struggling to bring the seat upright.

"Yeah. They're not so tough now we're shooting back. We probably surprised them back in Reading, thinking everyone else was evacuated. Why aren't they dead yet?" Dan questioned.

"They are, they just don't know it, like the kidnappers."

"Is Reading within the death zone yet? All we know is it was evacuated recently." Dan continued along the M4 in silence for a few kilometres. He frequently checked his mirror now. The pursuing van remained at a distance; sometimes going out of sight with the bends and dips in the road. Dan increased speed. He banged the steering wheel a few times when he couldn't lose them. "Next time we borrow a faster car."

After a few more kilometres, the van accelerated.

"I think they're going to make another run at us," he warned Nala.

Nala dropped her seat again, scrambled onto her stomach and took aim. She fired several shots. The van started swerving back and forth. The erratic driving increased. The van fishtailed, skidding off the road, through the fence and over the embankment.

"They've gone off the road."

Dan slowed quickly and did a U-turn. "Get ready just in case someone survived."

He drove the Mazda back, stopping a short distance from the busted fence. Below, the van was on its roof after rolling several times, as evident by the damage to the side panels. There was no sign of movement, only the ticking sound of the cooling exhaust when the light raindrops hit the hot surface.

"Cover me." Dan whispered, pointing for Nala to move behind part of the intact fence for protection.

She nodded and moved into position, gun ready and watching intently for movement.

Dan crouched and carefully slipped down the long, wet grass and approached warily. As he got closer, he stood up waved to her and advanced without a care.

"They're all cactus." He walked around to the other side of the vehicle. "You did hit the driver."

Nala scrambled down quickly to join him. What she saw wasn't surprising, considering the wreckage, but all occupants also showed signs of sickness.

"If anything, the crash was a mercy for them," she said.

Dan bent down out of sight for a moment, then he made his way around the car, returning with two gym bags. "This might come in handy." He showed her the bags of cash. It also had a couple of guns in it.

Nala shook her head and shrugged. "I guess."

"If we use our account or cred-chip, people can trace our movements. This makes us electronically invisible."

"Not that the new society will be using money. Money is only as good as the government — or corporation — issuing it, and in a few months none of those will be around."

"I know. Bartering instead will be the go; can't eat money ... But still, until then..." He zipped the bags and tossed each one up the embankment, then they helped each other up the slippery slope. Once back in the car and after using an old towel to dry off from the rain, the pair continued west towards Stonehenge.

"Do you think the druids and wiccans will still be out there?" Dan asked.

"It hasn't been that long. With no authorities to move them on, I dare say some will still be partying."

"I take it you're not a fan of the druids?"

"I'm sure they're good people, but all this 'spirituality' ... can't they just appreciate nature and the environment for what it is without trying to personify it by giving it a label or a face?"

"Maybe they just like parties."

CHAPTER FOURTEEN

"Isn't that one of those Reaper vans?" Nala pointed to the vehicle ahead, traveling east on the motorway. "I didn't realise they could move so fast."

They had entered the westbound lane of the A303 via the A34 on-ramp.

"It's a Reaper, alright." Dan recognised the squat, eight-wheeled all-terrain vehicle. "Did you know it's based on an old Aussie Defence vehicle? 'Bushmasters' they were called then, now with improvements to cope with plague-ridden areas including fully AI-controlled and all-wheel steering. That's the DIC logo and the configuration's similar to other Reapers. The last one I saw was the GHO one in São Lucas."

"What on earth is it doing out here? There's been no major deaths in the area."

"Good question. Maybe they heard about Winchester? It was DIC barracks, after all." He watched the van in the rear-view mirror veer smoothly to the off-ramp. "Yes. It must be. It's just turned onto the A34. That'll take them south to Winchester."

Barely decelerating, the vehicle whipped around the bend perfectly, as only an AI-controlled vehicle could. He could just hear the faintest squeal of the tyres.

Nala examined the Nav to view the roadmap. "And we've forty kilometres to go before Stonehenge. We'll be there in about twenty minutes."

"Good. I need to stretch my legs."

The rolling green hills and fields passed by, seen between the hedges growing along the roadside. Nala's phone pinged with an incoming message.

"A text from Rhyll. All went according to plan there. She's heading to Giza and should be there in several hours."

"Giza? The Egyptian pyramids?"

"Unless you know of another Giza."

"I—" Dan's phone rang.

Nala picked it up, thinking it might be Rhyll. She was disappointed. The number was listed as Brody Thurston. She activated the speaker.

"Hello. Dan Dobson?"

"Hey, Brody. What's up?" Dan spoke loudly.

"Can you see our drone? We lost signal a few minutes ago, after you joined the A303."

"Hang on. I'll pull over and take a look." Dan slowed and moved the car to the shoulder of the road. "Have you been monitoring all this time?"

"No. Conserving power. Why? Did we miss anything special?" Brody asked.

"A bank robbery in Reading. They chased us for a while, but died from this sickness."

"What on earth were they thinking?"

"No doubt thinking this death wave was a conspiracy." Dan stepped out of the Mazda and joined Nala by the fence. The ground was damp after a recent rain and a stiff wind blowing from the northwest bent the roadside weeds sideways.

Above, all they could see were the low clouds scudding from horizon to horizon.

"No sign of your drone anywhere," Dan called out over the breeze. "What do you think happened to it?"

"That model is extremely reliable. Even if it malfunctioned there'd be a homing signal."

"I gather there isn't?"

"Nada. The scope's completely dead." Brody paused. "If I had to guess I'd say it was hacked, but it's unhackable."

"These days, nothing connected to the network is unhackable; you'd just need an extremely good AI to work it, and only high-ranking corporations have that sort of tech. Which raises the question; who would, and why would they bother? If you covered anything they didn't want, they'd either blow it out of the sky, sue your arses, or simply buy you out."

"In either scenario, we'd still have a GPS signal."

"I—" Dan stopped as Nala shook his arm. They both heard whirring tyres getting louder.

In the distance, the Reaper came into view, racing down the A303 on-ramp towards them.

"What was that? You cut out there," Brody said.

"We have a Reaper coming towards this location," Dan said loudly.

"A Reaper? There's no reported deaths in the area."

"We thought it was heading to Winchester." Dan watched. When the Reaper wasn't a concern, it looked like poetry in motion, the way it negotiated bends and undulating terrain at speed; now that it was rushing towards them it looked like a predator coming in for the kill.

"I think we should step away from the road," Nala urged him over the fence.

Dan obliged without argument, staring at the oncoming vehicle. "There's no reason to be concerned. We're not dead ... the AI would detect that immediately and ignore us." He didn't sound overly convincing.

"I just did some digging. We've picked up a DIC communiqué; they reported several Reapers from their Salisbury depot went missing an hour ago. What are the chances our drone and these Reapers go missing in the same location?"

"Astronomical, I'd reckon." Dan and Nala stopped several

metres into the fallow field and waited.

Far faster than a human-controlled vehicle could accomplish, the Reaper decelerated smoothly and rapidly.

"Brody, it stopped. I think we'll be legging it for a while. Talk soon, but I'll keep the line open." Dan popped the phone into a pocket and looked around for an avenue of escape.

The field they were in was recently tilled, devoid of any growth, only long furrows to contend with.

"You wanted to stretch your legs." Nala pointed. "Let's stretch them in the direction of those trees."

Dan nodded, and they started running. Behind them they could hear mechanical noises.

"Any idea what that noise is?" Nala called. The ground was too treacherous to risk looking back.

"It sounds like the androids are deploying."

"I assume we should be concerned now?"

"Assume away." Dan concentrated on his footing as the soil was soft; it would be just too easy to roll an ankle. It took them several minutes to cross the field and reach the shelter of the trees. Once they were out of sight, they paused to rest and look back.

Like the droids in São Lucas, these were painted in the blue-and-white colours of DIC. Two of the androids were making their way across the field, following their path. They had dropped to all fours like dogs, crossing the soft soil with little difficulty.

"Those bots are following our footsteps." She glanced over her shoulder, seeing the obvious trail they left in the mud.

"Seeing ... our heat signatures ... more likely," he said, breathing heavily. "Infrared."

"Fuck! So they'd pick us up even now?" They had moved deep within the foliage.

Dan nodded, wiping his brow. "And the Reaper's gone somewhere, maybe to head us off."

Nala thought back to the roadmap she'd been studying. "There's several lanes near us. Assuming the Reaper continued in the same direction, there's a small village to the south ... Barton something, and a smaller one to our east."

"Which one's closest?"

"Barton something. We can hide in one of the houses if we're quick."

"I reckon they'll find us eventually."

"You know, it's times like this when the man is supposed to sound positive."

"I'm positive they'll find us eventually."

"Idiot." Nala punched him in the shoulder and continued through the undergrowth, heading south.

Dan followed in her wake, hearing her swearing in Portuguese.

They came to a small creek. Nala didn't hesitate as she splashed through; Dan winced at the thought of walking in cold, wet shoes.

"I'm getting a pair of gumboots next time," he muttered as he trod in the knee-deep water.

"You'd be better off getting runners," Nala called back.

"We *do* seem to be doing that more. I don't like running." Dan looked down, dismayed at his waterlogged shoes as he stepped onto the ground. He ran into the back of Nala, knocking her over on the slippery bank.

"Shit, Dan!" Nala hissed as she sprawled into the damp grass and underbrush. There were no serious injuries, but her shirt was ripped when her arm went through the bushes. "You run like you drive."

"Sorry. Why did you stop?" He bent down to help her up.

"You said thermal imaging. We can use the water to avoid them trailing us." She pulled her sleeve from the tangle of the bracken, ripping it even more.

"Good idea," he said, though he didn't look overly excited at returning to the water.

"Too bad about your shoes though." She slid the short distance back into the creek and moved upstream slowly, trying to be quiet.

The pair stopped after about fifteen metres when they heard the droids pushing through the foliage downstream. The bend and overgrowth was sufficient to keep them out of sight from one another. Waiting until the droids moved further away, the pair continued, but the creek became steadily overgrown with thorns.

Climbing out of the bed they continued south through the woods and soon came upon a grassy field and the back of a row of houses. To their far left was silence; to their right they could hear metal scraping.

"I reckon the Reaper's having a spot of difficulty negotiating the narrow lanes," Dan guessed.

"If it slows it down, all the better for us."

"Shall we go?" Dan urged, trying to stop shivering.

"We should wait to be sure."

Other than the sound of the Reaper scraping and driving over parked cars, the area closer to them was silent.

"Let's go." Nala bolted across the clearing.

Dan took a deep breath and followed, squelching at each step. It wasn't long before he was breathing heavily again. "I think I might need to do this more often."

Halfway across, they picked up the sound of a drone.

"Shit. Do you hear that?" Dan called to her, not daring to look back less he trip.

"Keep running!"

The line of houses had a brick wall separating the field from the back yards. Nala tried the first gate. It was unlatched and she went through, grimacing at the screech of unoiled hinges. Holding the gate from springing closed, she waited until Dan jogged through and checked the field before shutting the gate. It was still clear. She turned her gaze upwards.

"Does the Reaper have drones?"

"I don't know. It would seem likely, to spot the body placement in built up areas."

"Can their infrared reach through these walls?"

"I know the droids can, and can only assume drones as well,"

Dan panted. "Depending on the material and thickness."

"Well, that's just fucked-up!" Nala cursed. She pivoted and ran down the side of the house to the front, listening for the Reaper, while Dan came up behind her. The metal scraping sound was about a block away. "What are your thoughts?" she asked him.

Dan took a moment to consider the options while he caught his breath. "We'll have to stop the Reaper before we can get away. On the open road it'll catch us, and in the towns the droids will."

"To incinerate us?"

"I reckon it's been hacked and reprogrammed to capture us."

"Stradjek's doing?"

"I don't think he has the resources to hack military-grade AI. He much prefers getting henchmen to do thug work. That's what I was saying to Brody—" Dan remembered the phone in his pocket. "Brody, you still there?"

"... I am. You sound like you're in the thick of it."

Dan explained to him what they were up against.

"Those Reapers are designed for total automation and rugged localities. They are tough mothers to deal with, and then you have eight droids—"

"You aren't helping. How do we stop it."

"Sorry ... Wait ... My man here says he's only ever heard of one Reaper damaged in action. Moisture — water got inside."

"Oh. Easy. Just have to penetrate the hermetically sealed, armoured body. Great." Dan explained further to Nala: "The AI circuitry is very sensitive to moisture. And the interior's full of desiccant, or water-absorbing gasses. One of the reasons it's fully automated — even the condensation from the breath of human operators is sufficient to damage it."

"Correct."

They both heard the back gate screech open.

"Time to go!" Nala hissed.

"Talk soon." Dan popped the phone back into his pocket and followed Nala.

CHAPTER FIFTEEN

RHYLL AND NIELS MET FOR AN EARLY BREAKFAST BEFORE THEY GOT things underway. There was no need for Michal this time.

"If Stradjek does see the newscast, I've made some arrangement to help convince him." He then explained what had been organised with his workers and colleagues: increasingly obscure messages, then nothing, stopping production and transportation — basically giving everyone the day off, as long as they remained inside and out of sight, and with a few bodies for visual effect. "We even studied the data on the other death wave areas to make it look as authentic as possible. Given the remoteness of the mine, we should be okay."

"I can message Brody to splice or cut where needed. The bodies would be even more convincing."

"How long should we keep it going?"

"Until I'm certain my friends are safe. It could be a couple of days, but I'll let you know as soon as I can."

Niels sighed. "Sooner would be better, but I understand. Lucky we don't rely solely on the mine's production capabilities to keep it going."

"Do you trust everyone here?"

"Other than myself, they are all locals. I can vouch for their integrity."

Once breakfast was finished, Rhyll decided to try a little experiment based on what they'd only touched on earlier. She turned to face the arboretum, relaxed and concentrated on healing the plants within. Her method was much the same as when she healed physical injuries; sensing affliction and diverting energy to the area.

Admittedly the plants were in good condition already, but she wanted to see if there were any improvements. She also experimented while holding the diamond, to see if that made a difference.

"Do you see any change?" she asked Niels a few minutes later.

He got up to examine the garden closely. "I can't say for sure ..."

To Rhyll, there was a faint aura about the plants now — much like the grove near Stonehenge — but other than sensing good health, she honestly couldn't see much of a difference.

"Why not try outside?" Niels asked.

"I'm concerned the drone might pick it up, and therefore Tyrone might see it."

"Perhaps your reporter could splice that out too."

Rhyll got up and they stepped outside, but remained under cover of the terrace.

"What about that small garden?" Niels pointed to a dry section with too much shade.

Now that she was concentrating on it, Rhyll could feel the plants' distress — lacking water and nutrients — and repeated the process. After several minutes, they did appear somewhat healthier.

Niels' surprise was clear on his face as he slapped her shoulder lightly.

"It's a slight reprieve, and they will still need water," she replied to his compliment.

• • •

By midday, everything that could be done had been done; a few bodies randomly scattered around the compound had been recorded. Radio and vid-coms had been attempted, but failed due to severe static interference. Then: complete silence. Once that was accomplished, everyone was ordered to stay indoors and to relax until further notice.

"What if someone else sends a drone out to check?" he asked when he caught up with Rhyll. "They won't see any bodies, and we haven't got the capability to make dummies."

"Maybe we need the assistance of some of the local wildlife," she suggested.

"The powered fences keep them out, and it could take ages before wild animals choose to visit. They've learnt a long time ago to keep away."

"Then we need to open the gate. No guarantees, but I'll see what I can do to encourage them to visit. It can be argued the *missing* bodies were eaten or at least dragged away to a lair."

After a bit of consideration, Niels added to her suggestion. "We have paint and dyes; we can leave a 'blood' trail. I know just the person." He made a phone call to arrange it before he continued. "Obviously it wouldn't pass forensics or any bioscans, but a normal drone will see it as we want."

They strolled to his car and drove out to the main gate, where he used his ID to open it.

"I don't know if this will work." Rhyll wandered a dozen metres beyond the perimeter, relaxed and concentrated. In her mind, she called for her friends to come closer.

A few minutes of this summoning caused something within her to stir, something unexplainable; a presence or a power — something not her, but not alien, either.

Rhyll waited until the presence faded; it didn't leave her, but she sensed it returned to some deep place where it had been dormant. *Or is it dormant? Maybe it's been there all along and I've just not sensed it.*

"Niels, you better get back into the car, just in case," she said, spying movement on the low, sparsely foliaged hilltop.

"Wild dogs?" Niels was looking through his binoculars.

"*Lycaon pictus.* I suppose you expected *Panthera leo*? Perhaps *Acinonyx jubatus* or *Crocuta crocuta*?" Rhyll joined him in the car.

"Lions and cheetahs are much nicer to look at. Not too keen on ... Is that hyenas?"

"You know your animals."

"As I've been saying, it's what we do."

"For the moment, I'll take what I can get. Did you think of throwing in a few steaks and old clothes for atmosphere?"

"It was a suggestion from one of my people; she does drama class once a month."

Rhyll nodded with a smile as he turned the car around and they headed back to the building. Not long after, she grabbed her pack.

"Not staying for lunch?"

"I do need food to help re-energise ... maybe I can take something? Time is costing lives as it is. I can't thank you enough for your understanding and cooperation."

"And I'm relieved no one here is really dying. Thank *you* for that," he said as he escorted her to the arboretum, where lunch had already been laid out.

"Oh. Sorry for the wasted effort." Rhyll felt embarrassed at declining to eat; it looked delicious.

Niels spoke quietly to one of the staff, and within minutes a selection of food was sealed in a container.

"Don't worry, it's all vegetarian." Niels handed the container to her as they made their way back to the entrance. "Don't you need me to drive you to your hoverpod?" he asked as he shook her proffered hand.

"It's only a short walk. I'll be fine. Perhaps we'll meet again."

"If I survive," he replied as she opened the door.

Rhyll paused, concentrating. "You will, I have no doubt." She closed the door behind her and walked the short distance to the hoverpod. A couple of cheetahs skulked onto the scene. She paused as they approached and ruffed their necks and shoulders, before they sauntered off. She smiled and waved when she saw Niels watching from the window.

Back in the pod, she put her lunch down and messaged Brody. As she sat and waited for the drone to appear, she hit the green button and donned her headset.

The speakers crackled within a minute.

"Yes." The voice wasn't Stradjek's.

"Where's Stradjek?"

"He's very busy sleeping. Have you finished?"

"Job done. I need coordinates for Giza."

"The pyramids in Egypt?"

"Unless you know of another Giza."

"I'll punch through the coordinates. Sit tight. A message here from the boss in case he doesn't hear what he wants: the glide capabilities of the pod are zero."

The line went dead.

"Another bastard," she cursed. When she removed the headset, she heard the hum of a drone.

The cheetahs snarled and ran off at the noise when the drone landed beside the pod entrance.

As it shut down, Rhyll stepped outside, just as the pod fired up.

In a rush, she quickly grabbed the drone and jumped onto the retracting stairs. The motor whined in protest and they began unfolding again. She stepped inside the pod and the stairs, now free of obstruction, retracted.

Rhyll stowed the drone, sat down and watched the mine dwindle as the pod climbed and turned northeast towards Egypt. The monitor indicated the route with a dotted blue line. Giza was six hours away.

Once she'd relaxed and sipped some water, she tried to call her mother and Nala, but the phone signal here was now too weak.

"Hey, computer, can you place a call to a cell phone?"

"Authorisation required for outgoing communication."

"Please?"

"Authorisation not accepted. Unable to comply."

"Or else?"

"Authorisation not accepted. Unable to comply."

"Stupid computer!"

"Authorisation not accepted. Unable to comply."

"Probably recorded anyway." *Bastards.* Rhyll refrained from kicking it, and decided to text instead: *"Everything here went well and according to plan. I'm off to Giza in Egypt. I should be in the air for six hours. I'll let you know when I arrive."*

She caught up on the news headlines on the console display, seeing how much further the death wave had spread, and the rising death tally. The daily speed average might be slow, but it spread every hour of the day, non-stop, making her feel guilty with her rests, but she wasn't a machine. Her rest was vital.

In Brazil, the boundaries of the initial death wave from the mine and from Manaus had spread to a mere hundred kilometres apart at the time of her departure; the death toll was estimated at three million and expected to climb. She tried to calculate the deaths around the chakra points so far, and came up with over twelve million, based on the population densities she could find. Many people had managed to escape, even with all the chaos, but there was no mention of the numbers of survivors. It seemed the media still preferred broadcasting the bad news instead of the good.

Once the dire situation was realised, those areas with good communications fared better, being able to get word out to establish roadblocks and evacuate vast areas quickly; areas such as Mount Kailash in Tibet, and Uluru in central Australia, were both sparsely inhabited and communication was patchy at best, being so remote.

There was slightly better news with the reduced fatalities reported in the Lake Titicaca and Somerset regions, and she could only hope some of that was the healing work of the crystals. She managed to view a few snippets of the druid festivals for Samhain, and a few small, independent channels were still running Dan's report.

Rhyll's reading slowed as her eyes drooped.

The console beeped, flashing *"Incoming communication."*

She jumped at the unexpected sound. Knowing who it was, she wasn't going to relish the conversation. She put the headset on and listened.

"I see you're on the move and assume you have the diamond and did as you were told. I'm sure you're smart enough to know what will happen if I don't see a news report of the terrible tragedy. Once I see the broadcast, another diamond will be on its way and I'll send the coordinates of your next task."

"Where will that be? What colour is the next diamond?"

"I'll leave all that as a surprise. I wouldn't want you to think you can gain the advantage." Once again, the coms went silent.

"Arsehole." Rhyll placed the headphones in their holder. After a huge yawn, she went to wash her face before settling down for the remaining hours it would take to arrive in Giza. Her dreams were a mix of sword-wielding battles and swathes of land regenerating before her eyes at her will.

As she dozed, the console flickered briefly. Moments later, new coordinates appeared on the monitor, and the pod gradually turned from its designated flight path.

CHAPTER SIXTEEN

"Can't shake that damn drone!" Nala cursed.

They spent about ten minutes zigzagging from house to house of the quaint English village, over fences, through hedges and crossing back and forth across the road. Slowly, they made their way to the town centre.

"Any ideas yet?" she huffed as they rested.

"An army barracks with a tank would be handy. Or explosives."

"Can you drive a tank or handle explosives?"

"Nope ... but that's my idea."

"In the meantime, maybe we can lose them in those warehouses."

"Better than staying out here."

All the time they were moving, they could hear the sounds of the Reaper as it crashed into other vehicles in the narrow laneways. As they crossed the street, two more droids turned the far corner.

"Shit. More of them! C'mon, Dan." Nala increased her pace.

Dan managed to keep up, but it wouldn't last long. Other than his lack of condition, he was starting to get blisters from his wet shoes.

They skirted the high wire fence surrounding the compounded, glad the gates were still open.

"In here." She raced across the yard towards the nearest warehouse. The large doors were closed, but the small built-in door was ajar. Once Dan stumbled in, she slammed it shut and locked it. "Time for your insights."

"I'm fucked." He slumped onto a small stack of pallets, his breath labouring as he wiped the sweat off.

"That's deep, but no help. What can we do against these droids?"

"Barehanded against four? Not much. They're tough and resilient."

Looking for something to help, Nala started moving. The large interior was divided into several sections: two storage areas, a servicing bay, and a machine shop at the far end.

"You'll recall I mentioned something about being more positive?"

"That forklift could be useful," Dan noted as he walked towards it.

The door rattled behind them.

"We better come up with an idea soon. Can you drive a forklift?"

"I did when I worked in my father's print shop, but it was years ago and a completely different model."

"How hard can it be? It has forks and it lifts."

He jogged over to it. "Older model. No keys and no time to try hot-wiring it."

"And you know how to hot-wire the ignition?"

"Nope." Dan shook his head as the door rattled louder. The pair raced to the machine shop.

"Plenty of tools to play with here," Nala said as Dan joined her in inspecting the bench.

"You said they see infrared. What if we make things hotter?" Nala pointed to four barrels. "What do you think, oil or fuel?"

Dan nodded and raced over and worked the lid free as the entrance door started groaning. "Smells like oil." The first barrel was nearly empty. Repeating the process on the next barrel found a result. "Probably used sump oil, from its colour. Over they go." He put his shoulder to it and pushed. Nala added her strength and the heavy barrel toppled over.

Dark oil immediately splashed out over the concrete floor. Nala used her foot to roll the barrel, spreading the oil. The next barrel followed and as hoped, the lid popped with the impact, adding its contents to the large slick; the same with the third barrel. Dan then pushed it in the other direction with his boot, the pool of dark liquid now covering over half the width of the floor.

"Can you grab that extension cord?" he asked.

Nala looked to where he was pointing, a coil of electrical cord on a hook by the workbench. She brought it over, careful not to step in the spreading slick.

"Lighting it is one thing, but where do we go?"

"Out those windows. This should delay them, maybe confuse them. I hope." He hefted the cable, noting by its thickness it was a heavy duty three-phase cord.

Light stabbed across the floor as the far door was wrenched off its hinges.

They both crouched behind the first barrel as the silhouette of a droid stepped through the opening, followed by another. Using the barrel's bulk to hide his movements, Dan crept back to the bench and scoured for a knife to cut the plug off. All he could find was a small wirecutter. He cursed under his breath and started snipping.

Nala realised it was going to take a few minutes for him to be ready. She crept back and grabbed random tools from the untidy bench. She took aim and hurled a spanner into a far corner. Instantly the droids pivoted and moved in that direction.

"How's it going?" She risked a look at him.

"Slowly. Good throw."

"I can do this all day, but I'll run out of tools soon." Nala kept an eye on the droids. When they moved to one area, she threw a wrench into another corner. "They aren't too bright, and they're AI?"

"Not them, extensions to the AI inside the van. They are the AI's eyes, ears and muscle, but understand they were really designed to collect bodies. They're only sturdy because of the remote localities they need to work in. They could be removing bodies from a collapsed mine or building."

"Not just for purging, then?"

"One of the many adaptations." He snipped the last wire. "Done." The plug dropped to the floor and he now stripped the wires and spread them, making sure they didn't touch.

"Then why are these ones after us?"

"I can only assume some corporation has an interest in us."

"Dead or alive?"

"Preferably the latter. I think they're after a cure, some way to beat this death wave. They can't find Rhyll, so we're it."

"To be honest, distracting them from going after Rhyll is a good thing." Nala launched another tool just as a third droid appeared in the doorway. At first she thought she got away with it, but all three droids instantly turned in her direction, not towards the clatter of the tool. "Damn. I see what you mean about eyes and ears; one sees or hears something, the others instantly become aware too."

"Great tech," Dan said as the three droids marched towards them. "Sucks, doesn't it?"

"Let's hope that works." She inclined her head to the cord.

Dan stood and threw the extension lead into the spreading pool of oil before plugging it into the socket. "We're about to find out." He flicked the switch.

Nothing happened. Dan flicked the switch off and on again as the droids entered the workshop area. He then tried wriggling and twisting the cord as the droids moved closer. "You better get up onto the bench and open a window!"

Nala scored one in the face with a hammer before she turned and climbed the bench.

There was a loud zap. The wires finally shorted in the oil

pool, creating the necessary spark. The floor erupted in flames. Dan had to dive to the floor as the initial burst of fire leapt at the fumes.

The roar of the flames almost drowned out the sound of the smashing glass.

"Quick. Get up here!" Nala called.

Dan's hands were slick with oil, and climbing the bench was tricky. Nala helped drag him up. Since the windows were at bench height, the drop to the ground was barely over a metre. Dan went through first, and reached to help Nala, but she dropped to the ground like a cat.

They could hear the sound of another droid coming around the corner.

"This way," Nala hissed, moving in the opposite direction.

They could now see the yard contained five warehouses and a couple of smaller, office-like buildings. Two of the larger warehouses were side by side, with one now billowing black smoke. The three smaller warehouses to their right abutted each other, and the offices were ahead on the far side of the yard.

They ducked down the alley between the two long warehouses. The Reaper appeared at the far end of the alley, looking slightly battered from negotiating the narrow lanes.

"Back we go." Nala pivoted, almost running into Dan.

The pair sprinted across the yard to the smaller warehouses, heading to the nearest open door. Behind them, they heard the vehicle accelerate.

Inside was row upon row of boxes stacked high on pallets. Dodging between them, the pair raced to the far side. The windows here were out of reach and there was no other exit.

"I've an idea." Dan jogged back to a strange-looking device and started fiddling with it.

"What the hell is that?"

"Another type of lifter, I think. It's like a manual forklift." As he spoke, he pushed it so the forks were fully under the nearest pallet. He then turned a dial on the controller. There was a hum as the motor engaged, lifting the pallet up. The tone changed as the forks took the weight. When the load was a few of feet off the ground, he toggled the forks to angle forwards and down.

"Look out, it's going to topple." Nala tried to pull him back.

"That's the plan." Dan continued angling the forks. The column of boxes teetered, eventually succumbing to gravity and falling forward against the next stack. With a bit of judicial toggling of the forks, the second stack toppled. Like dominoes, the subsequent stacks began leaning precariously.

Two droids entered the warehouse. Dan yelled and waved at them to gain their attention. As they moved towards him, the collapsing stacks rained down, falling haphazardly and blocking the door; some landed on the droids and knocked them over.

"Meh. Not as good as I hoped." He dropped the controller and followed Nala, who was waving him to the far side.

"While they're busy here, let's see if we can slip into the next warehouse."

There were several doors along one wall. The first exit was locked, but the second one opened. This space was dim and dusty, containing a tractor and other farm machinery.

Dan jogged over to the tractor. "What are the chances of this working?" he muttered.

"Can you drive one of those, too?" Nala came up beside him.

"No, but how hard can it be? Motor, gears, brakes ..."

There was no key in the ignition. Looking around, he noticed the small cubicle in the corner. When he ran over, he saw the open key cabinet, grabbed the most obvious key and raced back.

Nala was sitting in the seat, with her hand out. "Four years helping the local villagers at home." She fired up the motor. "What was your plan?"

Dan shrugged. "I was just going to run over any droids I saw."

"Good enough." Nala engaged the gears and lurched forward towards the exit.

Dan jogged beside her. She slowed beside the large sliding door. He pulled it across. A blackened bot, paint peeling off its frame and looking the worse for wear, appeared in the window of the burning warehouse across the yard. It fell forward, crashing to the ground; with a whir of servos and much effort, it managed to right itself but was dragging one of its legs and an arm hung limp.

The Reaper parked at the front of the warehouse containing the toppled stacks. Two droids stood by it; one was pushing through the blocked warehouse door, while the other had turned to the approaching, damaged droid.

"There are too many of them to deal with at the same time."

"Let me worry about that." She patted her pocket. "I still have the gun. I'm sure you'll come up with something to assist." Nala surged forward out the door and turned towards the nearest droid as it confronted her. The damaged droid continued toward the van.

The odds were looking good until the one entering the nearest warehouse pivoted at the threshold of the door and moved in her direction.

She veered left; the droids turned with her. She veered right, so did they. She continued the turn and began to lead them down the alley between the two larger warehouses. The droids ambled after her as the drone buzzed overhead.

Dan watched, worried at first, but as the droids were led away he breathed a sigh of relief and scratched his hair. "How the hell do I take out an armoured AI?"

He jogged to the door of the next warehouse. More stacks of boxes greeted him, but his eyes lit up at the heavy-duty forklift. Urged by the sight of Nala trying to fend off droids single-handedly, he raced over to it. This was a newer model than he'd used previously, but it was a push-start, much like a car.

He jumped inside the cabin and ran his eyes over the controls. There was a slight whirring sound when he punched the start button. On the control panel, a series of lights appeared, blinking on and off as the machine went through the self-check sequence. A quick muck around with the controls was all he needed to get the gist of it. He drove the machine around inside the small space available to him to get a feel for the controls.

"Woohoo!" There was even a button to remotely activate the door, and he threw himself at the opening, barely clearing its underside as he rolled swiftly and silently through the gap.

Distant gun shots rang out.

"Shit!" he swore. Steering towards the van, the two droids turned to him. Dan raised and spread the forks as he aimed at the nearest droid. It was going to be close, as they both reached for him. He caught one between the forks and used the rear-wheel steering to spin around and slam the second droid into the side of the van. Using the thumbwheel on his armrest, Dan closed the forks as he lowered them, forcing the droid to be dragged along the concrete. Sparks flew as the metallic torso scraped on the harsh surface.

The forks squealed in protested as the droid tried to force them apart. Dan decided the next course of action and aimed for the nearest warehouse wall. Belatedly, he reached for the safety harness, managing to click it home as he ploughed into the wall.

The droid was pushed hard up against the sturdy frame of the forklift. Dan reversed and repeated running into the wall, crushing it again.

When he backed away and opened the forks, the droid dropped free, lying on the ground. It was still functioning, but barely. More shots were heard.

"No damned time to play!" He spun around, running over the reaching arm of the damaged droid and aimed at the van, raising the forks just over a metre. Like before, he pinned the next droid between the forks, this time ramming the side of the van and piercing the panel, the droid jammed between the two vehicles.

He couldn't tell if he'd had any significant effect. The van tried to move, but the weight of the forklift slowed it down. Manipulating the controls like a maniac, Dan attempted to inflict as much internal damage as possible. The forks twisted, moved up and down and widened, but the van eventually pulled free, tearing a large rend in its side. The droid in the forks dropped out of sight. The forklift bucked wildly as the wheels ran over it, and Dan would have been thrown out of the seat if not for the harness.

Dan swung the machine around and raced down the alley after Nala. In his rear-view mirror he spotted two more androids coming after him. Only one was free of any damage.

He maintained his speed, knowing he'd be overrun if he slowed down. At the end of the alley he swung to the right, almost rolling the forklift; not seeing which way Nala went, it was a fifty-fifty chance he'd find her.

A moment later he saw the tractor at an odd angle near the brick wall, with part of a droid visible underneath. Moving closer, he realised one of the rear tyres was flat, the android's arm broken off and protruding from the tread.

Nala was nowhere in sight but he did hear another shot. Skidding around the corner of the warehouse, he spotted her on top of a stack of empty pallets. A one-armed droid was trying to clamber up after her. She'd been shooting at it, but had just discovered she'd run out of bullets. Seeing the droid advancing, she nimbly jumped to the next stack and scrambled down the other side.

Reaching the top and discovering its target gone, the android dropped to the ground and began searching. Locating her departing figure swiftly, it gave chase.

Dan accelerated and ran it down; again the harness cut into his shoulders as the forklift heaved off the ground.

"Nala!"

She slowed and turned at the call. She pointed behind him. In the mirror he saw the Reaper bearing down on them from the far end of the yard.

"Jump on," he called as he screeched to a halt. The moment she had a handhold, he moved off again. "Get behind me and hang on tight."

"What now?"

"Now I think a cold shower is what is needed."

Nala shook her head at the nonsensical reply as he veered closer to the warehouse wall. She gripped tightly in apprehension, hearing the whirring of the Reaper's heavy tyres getting louder behind her.

"Whatever you do, do it quickly." No sooner had she spoken when her shoulders jarred as he careened into the side of the building. "What the f—"

The impact ruptured the water mains. High pressure water sprayed across the area, drenching them instantly.

The cold shock froze anything she was going to say.

Dan pushed the accelerator as hard as he could, urging the forklift to move faster, but after taking so much damage it was unresponsive; the front wheels were rubbing against the undercarriage and the motor had a high-pitched squeal.

The Reaper van shot through the torrent of water and closed in, as did three more droids from different directions. Two were in reasonable condition; the third was the fire-damaged one, dragging its leg.

The forklift finally died, leaving them exposed in the middle of the yard.

"Climb!" Nala grabbed a heavy-duty wrench from its housing under the seat, tossed it onto the narrow forklift roof, and scrambled after it. She reached down to help Dan. There was little room for the two of them, but the thought of grappling with droids was enough encouragement.

The droids spasmed, then froze, as they reached the forklift. The Reaper vehicle careened out of control, sideswiping the forklift and taking out two droids before it ploughed into the warehouse. The forklift tilted, knocking Nala to her knees just as she grabbed Dan, stopping him from falling back. He managed to get hold of the roof edge as the forklift righted itself. With her help, he clambered onto the roof, then helped her up.

They turned to watch the remaining droid warily.

"What just happened?" she asked. They both jumped when the drone crashed to the ground, sending bits of plastic and circuit boards flying in all directions.

Dan looked stunned for a moment. "I guess some of the water got into the AI system. Shorted it."

"Clever you. Is it dead?"

The Reaper was immobile. They could see sparks and hear crackling coming from the interior.

"Out of commission, enough to not be any more of a hindrance is my guess."

"Great. Now I could do with a hot shower." She shivered in her wet clothes in the cold air.

CHAPTER SEVENTEEN

"Zera, play news," Tyrone commanded his personal AI. "Search for Niger." The TV came to life and after a couple of seconds a report on Global News Network aired. It depicted aerial footage from a drone over the old mine. A couple of bodies could be seen. The caption *"Breaking news — mysterious death wave hits Niger"* flashed along the bottom of the screen.

"Finally, some success." Stradjek smiled. "I didn't think the girl had the stomach." Now all he had to do was ensure she still considered her friends were in danger. Still, if he had to arrange for her mother to have an accident ...

In a rare and spontaneous display of trust, he arranged for the next diamond to be sent immediately.

"Incoming message."

Tyrone put the pillow over his head and rolled over.

"Incoming message," Zera repeated.

He blearily looked at the clock. 02:17.

The pillow sailed across the room at the monitor, which toppled back against the wall. Tyrone sat up in his bed and yelled at the AI: "Damn it, Zera. Do you need an upgrade? What don't you understand about 'Do not disturb'?"

"Emergency call, Tyrone."

"Put it through," he said eventually. Rubbing his eyes, Tyrone reached for his robe and sat on the edge of the bed.

"Sorry to disturb you, Mr Stradjek. We've lost the pod and the girl."

"What? Speak up, man!"

"We've lost the pod and the girl."

Tyrone stomped over to the monitor and pulled the pillow off the speaker. "Damn it, Williams. How? Where the fuck has she gone?"

"Sir, we believe the pod has been hacked. We lost contact a couple of hours into the flight. It was travelling east over Niger at the time."

"And no trace at all?" Tyrone tossed the pillow back onto the bed.

"Nothing. The transponder signal has been cut completely. If there's any course change, we don't know it."

"So, you can't track it?" He paced back and forth, flustered at the early morning call, but more irate at the news. "Do we know who could do this? That AI pod was top of the line."

"Numerous entities come to mind—"

"And who's out to get me or knows what I'm up to? The Easterners? Did one of the mining corporations get wind of it? Maybe Franke sabotaged it?"

"If Franke sabotaged it, we'd still have the transponder. Those things don't simply cut out, there are too many fail-safes and if it crashed, even blew up, the emergency beacon would be pinging. As to who — many entities have the ability, but it's unlikely they'd worry about us. We aren't that big a concern."

"Not yet. What about ICON? Would those bastards get involved? They're not into mining, but we've crossed paths recently."

"If ICON is involved, perhaps they're merely doing it for a third party — someone who's into off-world mining and using them. Of course, it may have nothing to do with mining; perhaps a corporation is after a cure? Or someone is simply after the diamonds — they do represent a substantial windfall for an audacious mind."

Tyrone poured a bourbon and sat down, thinking. "You're certain the pod was hacked? Could this brat have done something?"

"As you say, it's top of the line AI. I doubt she has the knowledge to override the whole system at once. No, this is definitely an external source."

"Have we got a list of ICON interest and their partners?" He switched on the TV to get world news as he waited. There'd be no sleep tonight, and he wanted to make sure she had actually carried out her job after all. "I knew it was too good to be true," he muttered.

"I can compile a list, sir."

"Send it to me. What about our kidnappers in the UK?"

"They're still in Reading, or the phone is, but it did move slightly before we lost it."

"How did we lose the signal? Was that hacked too?"

"Highly unlikely. I can only assume the battery is dead."

"Fuck! Can't anything go right for once? What the hell were they doing in Reading? Weren't they supposed to rendezvous in Maidstone?"

"We've no information. Reading is on the way to Maidenhead. Maybe they're too sick to continue, or a double-cross?"

"Send a drone out to check," Tyrone ordered.

"Sir, we can try. Our influence over there is minimal, and any local assets have either been evacuated or died recently."

"Keep tabs on the phone anyway. If it pings in a safety zone, I want to know! Have you anything at all to report about the pod before we lost contact?"

"Just before arrival we have an indication of the door opening prior to landing. Could mean anything, but nothing to do with the hacking. Everything was nominal on departure."

"Is she after me? Does she know of my location?"

"Unlikely, in both cases."

Stradjek cancelled the call when his tablet pinged; the list of ICON affiliates arrived. He read the list. It was long, and some of the listed affiliates were shared between ICON and Volaris and several other organisations with mutual dealings.

He strongly considered a leak.

After a brisk walk to the Barton Stacey village centre, Dan went into the only pharmacy in town and grabbed antiseptic and bandages.

"I don't know how your feet can handle running in wet shoes," he complained. As he put the bandages in his pocket, he discovered the forgotten phone, but the battery had died.

"What can I say. A lifetime of living in the Amazon toughens you up in more ways than one," Nala replied.

They then began the search for accommodation. The town was too small for a hotel, but they came across a cosy bed and breakfast off the main street. The front door was unlocked.

"Seems nice enough," Dan said.

"I'm grabbing that hot shower," Nala said, disappearing down the hall.

Dan found a charger for the phone in the kitchen and started brewing a pot of coffee while he waited.

As soon as Nala finished, he took his turn.

Nala grabbed his clothes and shoes; she shoved them into the drier with hers.

Once warm and clean and sitting at the kitchen table in bath robes, they took the opportunity to snack on what food they could find.

There was now enough charge on the phone for a call to Brody to update him on the outcome. He congratulated them in surviving and confirmed another drone was on the way and should arrive shortly, believing the druid interview was still paramount.

"We should get out of here as quickly as we can, in case they send another Reaper," Dan suggested after he finished the call.

"You think they will? Are we worth that much hassle?" Nala helped take care of his blisters using what he pinched from the pharmacy and the first aid kit she found under the sink.

"Want to stay and find out?"

"I'll pass." She carefully slipped his shoes back on. "How's that?"

"Much better." Dan was trying to be stoic and not limp as he walked across the kitchen.

"Good enough to walk back to the motorway?"

"Ha. You can, but I'll be driving."

Finding and acquiring abandoned cars was also becoming routine. The most recent acquisition was an old Land Rover four-wheel drive.

"Why is this better than the Volvo? It was as old as this." Nala wrinkled her nose at the smell of the ancient interior as she climbed inside.

"I'm taking into account the recent Reaper hacking. This one isn't connected to any network and too old to have anything more than basic microchips. Unhackable."

"So old that it still uses diesel." Nala pointed to the fuel gauge. "There's a few drums back at the warehouse. Near that stack of pallets where you found me."

The pair drove back to the yard. The Reaper van and droids were still where they left them.

"That looks promising. No self-repair," Dan observed.

"They can do that?"

Dan shrugged. "Depends on the extent of damage."

They found the drums and manage to fill the tank but the old hand pump took ages. Nala scanned the skies while Dan worked the pump.

"All done," he said a quarter of an hour later.

"And all clear here."

They jumped back into the car and Dan drove the ancient vehicle to their abandoned Mazda on the A303 to retrieve their gear before continuing the remaining distance to Stonehenge.

"I can see smoke." Nala pointed. The ancient monument in the middle of the expansive field was easily visible from the road.

"No doubt the festival's still in full-swing."

"I'm not so sure. I can't see any people. Some of the marquees have toppled."

Dan glanced across; sure enough, the monument did look abandoned. "And some marquees have blown across the field, too."

They followed the road to the entrance and, as before, drove past the tourist car park to where many of the druids' cars were still parked in the nearby field. With nobody about, Dan drove right up to the charred remnants of the main marquee, which was tilted to one side, two of its legs buckled and wisps of smoke still rising from the smouldering canvas.

"Where is everyone, and why leave their cars?" Dan questioned. He reached for his camera.

They both climbed out to explored the chaos.

"Check these out." Nala walked towards the standing stones. She was looking at deep, wide tyre tracks.

"If I had to guess, I'd say a Reaper van came through here." Dan walked up beside her, camera aimed at the tracks.

"And these are droid footprints." Nala was following the many tracks, deep depressions in the damp ground of where the heavy androids must have passed. "I imagine those things weigh well-over a hundred kilos?" The droid footprints went in all directions. "Looks like they were chasing anyone they could."

"I can hazard a guess they were after them because they survived, like us."

"So we weren't being targeted specifically? That's a relief ... sort of."

Dan shrugged and went off at a tangent towards the side pavilion where he'd been practically force-fed a meal. He was now videoing the destruction. The tables were overturned and the food spoiled, strewn across the grass. He scanned the surrounding area in case someone had witnessed their return, but there were still no people to be seen, only the random shoe stuck in the mud or shawl lying on the ground.

Nala came over to join him after searching through the other pavilions. "There are more Reaper tracks over there, and there." She made sure she avoided getting in his documentary.

"At eight droids per machine, that's a lot of druids taken."

"Surely they didn't take them all? Where'd they put them?"

"I don't know, but there's no one left here."

"Let's hope they were smart enough to get away. I didn't take note of how many cars there were to compare now."

They looked up at the sound of the drone overhead.

Dan pulled the phone out of his pocket and dialled Brody. "I'm assuming that's you? Can you see?"

"Are those Reaper tracks?" Brody was heard over the speaker.

Dan told him all he could. "We've not seen or heard anyone. The place is completely abandoned. From your view, though, can you tell where they've gone?"

"No. The tracks all merge at the entrance. The mud trail on the bitumen wears out soon after."

"In and out the same way. We know they didn't go east on the A303."

"Salisbury is south. That's where the DIC depot is that lost the Reapers in the first place."

"Isn't that still within the zone? How far out are the boundaries now?"

"Allowing for a few days leeway, they now extend eighty miles with Stonehenge and Glastonbury as its centres."

"How far is London from here?"

"The CBD is about 95 miles."

"That's pretty close isn't it? *Miles* always confuse me. I'm surprised the UK hasn't gone metric."

"At the speed the wave is moving, they have just shy of a

week before it hits. It's being evacuated as we speak. All roads north are packed, as are the trains."

"Evacuating over twenty million people? Must be total chaos." Nala shook her head at the thought.

"If Salisbury is in the zone, how the hell did the death wave get to Reading so fast?"

"I'm not sure it did. Reading was evacuated a couple of days earlier. I think your kidnappers caught whatever this is back in Basingstoke. The last known area where we actually lost people before full evacuation was in Overton. Then Winchester somehow spontaneously started."

"Ah ... okay." Dan and Nala looked at each other, not willing to reveal Rhyll had started that by herself.

"I say, the drones just picked up a Reaper heading your way from the south. It will be at the 'henge in a few minutes."

"Shit." They said in unison, and started running to their car.

"Do you know where the closest evacuation point to us is?" Dan called.

"That would be ... Cheltenham. Directly north."

"That Reaper will catch us easily," Nala reminded Dan.

"On the road it will, that's for sure. Brody, the Reaper's much faster on the road, but if we go paddock-bashing with a head start and your drone's guidance, we might have a chance of staying in front. I don't think it will pursue us into a populated area."

They jumped into the Land Rover. After Dan placed the camera in Nala's lap he accelerated away in high-range, four-wheel drive, tyres kicking up sods of grass as they churned across the fields.

"I get you." There was a pause. "I've looped the pilot into this call. He'll direct you."

Nala held the phone while the pilot gave directions to avoid the worst obstacles. They raced north across fallow fields, mowing down gates and fences and bouncing through creek beds. A couple of times the Reaper surged ahead using the roads, but with the pilot's guidance they averted any potential ambush.

They played cat and mouse for over three hours before the Reaper stopped following them and turned back south. As the Land Rover crested a hill, Cheltenham could be seen below.

"Do you think it stopped, knowing it was too close to the safety zone?" Nala kept watching just in case.

"I was counting on it. Too many witnesses." Dan grimaced as he stretched. He had been tense and hunched over the steering wheel for too long. "I also think a chiropractor is in order."

The personnel at the official roadblock were a combination of DIC and local police. Beyond the barriers were several large vehicles, one in particular with the DIC logo. At first Nala and Dan were wary, but soon realised the DIC personnel knew nothing about either of them.

The pair were ushered into a portable decontamination unit much like the entry point to the GHO vehicle, with the disinfectant blast and UV lighting.

"I reckon the commander at Winchester went rogue," Dan whispered to Nala. "They don't know anything about it, or us."

"I agree," she said. "There's no way DIC would be leaving us alone if they thought we had anything to do with what happened there."

After their decontamination they were escorted to the Leckhampton police station and interviewed. When the senior constable realised who they were, he looked them up and down curiously.

"You won't find six fingers," Dan jested.

"How soon can we get out of here?" Nala asked him.

"As you may be aware, the roads are a shambles with the evacuation. All townsfolk are heading to Birmingham or further north. We're planning on the city being empty in two days. You're welcome to stay here and come with us then, but I saw you on the telly. I thought there were three of you?"

"We've been separated from our colleague." They explained about their kidnapping, and the fate of the kidnappers.

"If this Tyrone Stradjek is involved as you say ... I can't promise if or when anything will be done, him being out of our jurisdiction. If the kidnappers are dead and you have no direct evidence ... there's little we can do anyway."

"Wait a minute." Dan showed him the pics on his burner phone with the messages.

"I'll need to keep the phone as evidence."

"Here's the original phone from the kidnappers." Dan put his phone away and pulled out the sealed bag with phone, battery and SIM.

"We'll get our communications team onto it. No promises though, and it could take a while under the circumstances."

"We understand," Nala conceded.

"Sir, since you know who we are, you know we are immune to this death wave. What say you let us head to London instead? We have contacts there that can help us get back to Rhyll." Dan was lying, but the police were none the wiser.

The policeman considered their request. "It's no concern of mine, and I have enough on my plate. I suggest you leave it until evening though; less people out and about to see, therefore less chance a desperado will try to follow thinking they can get away with something." His radio squawked at him. "I'll get back to you tomorrow." He turned away to answer the call, but stopped. "You might be interested to know about half a dozen people came through a couple of hours ago. They also claim Reapers came after a group of them."

"Were they druids?"

The senior constable nodded with a chuckle, then continued with the radio call.

Shortly after, a corporal caught up with them and gave them two keys and a pamphlet with directions to the Lypiatt House Hotel and the assurance they'd be looked after.

CHAPTER EIGHTEEN

A CONSTANT BEEPING WOKE DAN. HE LOOKED AROUND, STILL groggy from sleep, and couldn't work out what it was. His back still ached and he was happy to stay under the warmth of the doona. The beeping continued incessantly. When he looked for it, the phone wasn't where he'd left it, the vibration causing it to fall from the bedside table. Grumbling, he rolled his upper body over to grope for it on the carpet and felt an arrow of pain down his stiff torso. He rolled onto his back with a hiss.

"Dobson," he croaked when he finally answered.

"It's Brody. I have some interesting news. We found our drone."

I got woken up and risked spinal injury for this crap? "The one near Stonehenge? I'm so happy for you. Bye—"

"No, wait. Not that one, the one we sent with your girl, Rhyllien."

"What? Where? When?" Dan sat up, quickly regretting it with the protest from his back.

"It's in Sedona."

"Where the hell's Sedona?"

"Arizona, Western Union. One of our underlings only reported the data a few minutes ago."

"How did it get there?"

Brody reminded Dan of the piggyback with Rhyll's pod.

"Getting to Sedona is going to be tricky." Dan attempted stretching, gently twisting side to side, to little avail.

"I dare say, what with the evacuations and all ..."

"Know of any unused hoverpods?" Dan chuckled as a joke. "Thanks for that, Thurston. Leave it with me. I'll let Nala know. Perhaps she can come up with something." Dan considered Nala's links with Imogen and the university as he slid the doona off and tentatively stood up. The phone remained silent. "You still there?"

"Uh yes, I was thinking of something ..."

"You know of a pod? I was joking."

"Actually, I can help with that too—"

"Help with getting a pod? You're kidding. Where?"

"It doesn't matter." Brody hesitated. "Much too difficult—"

"I want to know anyway. Maybe I can work something out."

"Well ... it's at our studio ... in Salisbury."

"Sals— Isn't that's where the Reapers are?"

"I believe so. Hence my hesitation. Street cams in most of that area are down, probably hacked too, so we can't be certain."

"Surely it's secured. We couldn't access it even if we got there ... could we?"

"I think I could arrange it ..."

"There's a but, isn't there?"

"Tell me more about Reading."

"Reading?"

"This bank robbery. You said the robbers came after you but died?"

"They did ..." Dan realised where this was going.

"I assume they had their takings with them?"

"One could assume that."

"Did you happen to grab it?"

"What if I didn't?" He thought he'd try Nala's argument. "Money will be pointless in a few months."

"Perhaps, but either way, better to have it than not, wouldn't you say? And if you didn't, it's not as if anyone else was going to grab it."

"What exactly do you want, Thurston?"

"Twenty-thousand pounds should do it."

"I see. I must say I'm disappointed."

"Because you wanted to keep it for yourself? Let's not be too altruistic about this. Even if you didn't take it, you thought about it."

"How will I get it to you?"

"We have courier drones that will suffice. Once you've done your bit, I'll send the activation codes to the pod."

"I'll get back to you." Dan cancelled the call. He needed a hot shower, breakfast and a strong coffee. Before his shower, he called Nala to let her know they were leaving.

She joined him for breakfast downstairs, dropping her bag next to his pack.

"Great news about Rhyll, but what an asshole Thurston turned out to be," she fumed when he told her the news. She had a towel with her and rubbed her wet hair vigorously.

"Yeah ... an opportunist, as much as I was, I guess. In hindsight, I did say it would come in handy." Dan poured the coffee for both of them and they started eating.

"We need to get to Rhyll." Nala lifted her mug and breathed in the coffee aroma. "What are we going to do?"

"I don't know how she got to Sedona, but I'm sure it wasn't her idea. She was headed for Egypt."

"Not part of Stradjek's retaliation for thwarting his kidnapping plans?"

"Who knows? Last we heard, she had accomplished the set task — and what happened in Niger was verified on the news."

"I'm surprised she went through with it." Nala looked disappointed, picking at her fruit slices.

"She's done it before for less. You think she'd hesitate with our lives on the line?"

Nala shook her head. "I hate to think what this is doing to her. She's still just a kid."

"All the more reason to get to her if we can. If it costs twenty thousand pounds, then so be it."

"Easy when you've got it, but I agree: this needs to be done."

Dan called Thurston back.

"Okay. We'll do it."

"Shall I send the courier drone to your coordinates in Cheltenham?"

"You can guarantee the pod control?"

"I have the codes as we speak."

"You do?" Dan thought they'd have to go to Salisbury to get the pod, but if Thurston had the codes, the pod could just as easily be remotely controlled, too. He wracked his brain for a nearby location, and quickly checked the map on his tablet.

"Send it to Seven Springs, just south of Cheltenham, next to the A435 and A436 roundabout. We'll exchange the money there for the pod and the codes, or the deal's off."

"You have got the money with you! My opinion of you has been restored. Let's make it thirty for the VIP pod and you've got a deal."

Arsehole. "Fine. What if this courier drone gets hacked like your previous one?" Dan asked.

"That's my concern and I'll see what I can do. No drone, no money. Agreed?"

"We'll be there around midday. Oh, and this call's recorded. If anything happens to us, the cops will get a copy." Dan hung up. "You still okay with this?" he asked Nala.

"Why are we still talking? The roadblocks will be trouble, or are you going cross-country again?" She drained her coffee and pushed her empty plate away.

"No need to go cross-country, and no, they won't be a problem. Remember the senior constable when I suggested London? He said he didn't care. If I hit him up for it, he might get the roadblock to open for us." Dan stood up.

"Sounds good." Nala hefted her bags. "I'm ready. Want me to take your bags old man?"

"She'll be right." Dan braced himself as he reached for his pack. His back twinged in protest.

The pod and drone were hovering at a hundred metres above them when they arrived at the location.

Nala remained in the car, gun ready, not that she thought it would be any use against a drone.

Assuming there was vid surveillance, Dan had already separated the cash so Thurston wouldn't see how much was left. He stepped out of the car and walked to the clearing.

The courier drone, larger and more powerful than the vid drones he'd seen earlier, lowered to a metre off the ground.

His phone rang.

"Show me the money and place it in the receptacle." Brody was hard to hear over the drone's buzz.

Dan reached into the bag and brandished six wads of cash, flicking through them.

"Five thousand each." He dropped them into the bag. "Land the hoverpod, open the door and send me the codes."

The pod dropped to the ground and the door swung up. His phone pinged with the codes. Dan turned and waved to Nala. She slipped the gun into a pocket, transferred their luggage from the car to the pod and climbed in before he placed the money in the drone.

The drone's buzzing increased before it shot into the sky and headed east.

Dan hung up and walked to the pod. "All set?" he asked Nala.

"If this is an upgrade, I approve. I've entered the coordinates. Everything seems okay. Do you think he'll double-cross?"

"No. He wanted the cash and he got it. He's an arsehole, but I don't think he's a vindictive arsehole." He turned to the console and closed the doors. "Computer, take us to Sedona, Western Union." He read out the codes.

"Passcode confirmed."

"ETA to set coordinates?"

"Arrival time will be 10:25 MST."

"Define MST."

"MST — Mountain Standard Time."

"That will be the local time zone. It's just over twelve hours. Plenty of time for coffee." Nala pulled out the thermos and their travel mugs.

There were four seats in the VIP hoverpod with inbuilt massage programs, which Dan utilised almost constantly during the long flight. The interior was luxurious, and the shower receptacle had everything you could want.

"You know, it would cost more than we paid Thurston to get first class tickets on any flight?" Dan smiled as he also found it had a minibar. He sank into the seat again, careful not to spill his drink, and reclined.

"We won't tell him." Nala was reading the news and about Sedona. "Sedona is renowned for some weird phenomena, including UFO sightings, strange energy fields and people going missing. Some swear it heals them, and it looks like every second building is either a health spa, meditation centre or alternate church of some sort."

"It's sounding like Rhyll would blend in easily," Dan murmured. "I hope she's still there by the time we reach her. Any reply to your texts?"

Nala shook her head. "I tried calling, but it doesn't even ring. I've kept Imogen up to date. She's not impressed, nor surprised, about Stradjek, but agrees this is not like him. She thinks it might be ICON."

"ICON, again?" Dan opened his eyes. "What else did she say?"

"They are well-connected, with an almost unlimited credit account."

"Why would they be after her? If they have that much credit?

No ... I know. Greed. They only got that wealthy by ruining any competition that got close, or by grabbing anything that others could use and using it for themselves. At first I thought they were merely after the diamonds."

"You have to admit, over a billion credits in diamonds isn't something to be sneezed at."

"Oh, I know. I think it's more than that now."

"How do you mean?"

"You and I know there is no cure per se to the death wave. I wouldn't put it past them to think they can find one, given unlimited resources. If not a cure, they'll want to find out exactly what is happening and why. They'll make sure there's a profit in this for them and their shareholders. If they succeed, they'd have a monopoly over everyone. That could make them *the* most powerful corporation in the world!"

"I wonder if we can set them onto Stradjek?"

"To divert them from Rhyll? Nice idea, but they have the resources to handle both with ease. Stradjek might be a pain to us, but to them it's the equivalent of a mozzie attacking an elephant."

"I wonder why it took them this long to make a move."

"Planning. They don't jump in like Stradjek. If the death wave is killing everyone in its path, they'll endeavour to find out how and why, then devise a strategy to thwart it, or make the most of it until they do."

"Sounds like they're ruthless."

"There's a reason they're one of the largest corporates in a corporate world."

"How do we compete with a global corporation?"

"Honestly? We can't. We just have to outlive them. A live pauper is still richer than a dead billionaire."

Hours before they arrived, Dan had managed to contact local TV and media outlets, explaining who they were and the purpose of their visit. Gobsmacked at garnering overseas interest from UKTV, representatives from TV and radio stations fell over themselves to offer assistance and were going to send out their own reporters and local personalities to escort them.

Landing was straightforward once the credentials of the VIP hoverpod was verified as a registered UKTV vehicle. Dan was about to explain his story to the authorities when the media entourage arrived in a loud and colourful flurry.

"The world will soon know about the mysterious vortices of Sedona. This will put us on the map!" their spokesman decried as he spoke enthusiastically to the uniformed officers. With his influence, Dan and Nala were ushered through quickly and given special treatment.

"Who is this clown?" Nala whispered as the spokesman was speaking to the security officers.

"According to the website, he's Max Imum," Dan whispered back. "I know, a name suitable for a clown; he *is* full-on. I'm glad we researched before we landed." Feeling so good after many hours of massage and minibar access, Dan was inclined to grab her luggage as well, but a couple of the junior staff in the entourage offered their services.

The pair were escorted to a chauffeured limo.

"To the L'Auberge de Sedona, my man," Max said to the driver as he opened the door for Nala. "It's the best five-star hotel in town."

"You realise we'll have to pay for all this?" Nala mentioned quietly to Dan as he climbed in behind her.

"Of course." Dan had taken the precaution of secreting the cash around his luggage, as well as keeping a decent sum on his person. Part of his plan was to tip generously as a distraction.

"We will not hear of it. Leave all this to us," their host, overhearing the conversation, interjected. "I'll get my team to do an itinerary for you. There's so much to see here, so many weird and wonderful things, and since Area 53 started, that's doubled."

"Area 53?"

"Oh yes ... but we certainly don't want to get the nasty reputation of Area 51. Too many crazies out there. Sedona is different, a spiritually uplifting environment. We are too dignified here for all that conspiracy-theory riffraff."

"Has word of the death wave reached here?"

"That? Oh yes. Terrible. We will be fine here, though." Max nodded with a smile.

"I'm glad to hear it." Dan sounded dubious. "We've already done a fair bit of research into it. It's quite devastating. So many are dying—"

"Oh, I'm sure it is a tragedy to the rest of society, but as I say, in Sedona we're extremely in tune with our environment, all that is and all that will be. Besides, I'm sure those in Area 53 are onto it and, they'll make sure we're safe here."

"Who are *they* in Area 53? Is it a new corporation?"

"We don't know, but we know they're there; we know they move among us, and we definitely know they pay generously. It's been a real economic boon having them."

"Sounds very fortunate—"

"No, no! Not luck at all. It's all part of being one with the universe. This is why we know this death wave will simply pass us by."

Nala gazed out the window, amused by this person. Of course, anyone else would no doubt consider their talk about adapting, resonating with Mother Nature, equally amusing. She hoped he was right, for all their sakes.

"This is an extraordinary landscape," she noted, in an attempt to change the subject. What she said was true: the landscape was spectacular, but her comment was also meant to prevent Dan from putting his foot in it. She'd known him long enough to see the signs of a witty retort about to ruin everything.

"Yes. Isn't it amazing? These mesas and rock formations go back millions of years ... I'll make sure a full tour is part of your visit." Max then went on in detail about all the lookouts and some of the more spectacular peaks. The car pulled into the drive of the hotel.

"Here we are, *Dudley*," the chauffer announced loudly.

Max stopped, managing to remain calm at the interruption. There was a second he held his breath, then he opened the door and the tirade started again as he began pestering the bellhops and concierge. His constant voice finally faded as he went inside.

Dan remained behind to talk to Chuck, their driver. "Dudley?" he asked.

"Dudley Smyth is his real name. Doesn't fit in with his ego though, so *Max Imum* he calls himself. You might be able to tell I'm not a fan of the Dud." Chuck laughed.

Dan slipped him a fifty credit note with a grin. "Thanks for that, Chuck. What can you tell me about Area 53?"

"The Dud is right when he said they are an economic boon. A lot of creds flowing now."

"Any idea who's running it?"

"Beats me." Chuck shrugged. "Government, I reckon, or the corporates, which is the same thing really."

"And where is it, or is that a secret too?"

Chuck laughed. "If it is, it's the worst secret in history. It's under the airport." He walked onto the grass area adjacent to the foyer entrance. Dan followed as the chauffeur pointed back the way they came. "See, the airport is on top of that plateau. I don't know how big it is, but this secret base is inside that."

"And the entrance?"

"On the southeast side, but I wouldn't go snooping about. While everyone jokes about it, they're deadly serious when it comes to security. People, generally tourists, go missing a lot around here ... or some fall off cliffs while *bushwalking*, if you get my drift. My cousin runs Scenic Air Tours. There's several benefits in doing a scenic flight; you'll see a hell of a lot more in a short time, and some of the best sights aren't accessible by road; an evening flight is spectacular too, and the Dud is terrified of flying, if you get my drift."

"Thank you for that." Dan slipped Chuck another note. "I'll be sure to give it a try."

Chuck gave him his card. "If you need a lift, or get sick of that clown and want a real tour, call me."

Dan checked the card. "No worries. Cheers."

Chuck climbed back into the limo and left with a wave. Dan nodded and went inside to rescue Nala.

CHAPTER NINETEEN

RHYLLIEN SLOWLY REGAINED HER SENSES, ONLY NOW BECOMING aware she had been numb. She opened her eyes. *Where am I?* Her legs, arms and torso were strapped, and she was wearing a short, white hospital gown. Her head throbbed, as did everything else. Looking down, she saw tubes attached to her arms. They disappeared out of sight under the bed; one of them looked like those used for blood transfusions. She could hear soft, rhythmic sounds and feel a slight vibration. *What the hell?*

The interior of the luxury pod had been replaced by grey walls and ceiling. The room was uniformly illuminated with concealed lighting. Three walls were devoid of anything but light panels, but the fourth had a long, low window. In the other room she saw a table with monitors on top, but she could only see the back of them. It was dimmer, but she saw movement of people in gowns like those worn by medical staff, but theirs were pale blue. It was hard to tell with the glare, but there appeared to be several black-clad soldiers against the back wall.

As the feeling returned gradually, she wished it hadn't; the pain became excruciating. Rhyll felt her anger and stress rising as the pain increased. *People are going to die.*

An uncomfortable sensation came from her groin. Without

the capability of movement, she thought she was wetting the bed. It took her a moment before it dawned on her. "They inserted a fucking catheter!" she croaked, her throat dry. *Bastards.*

A door swished open. Turning her head was painful. Everything was painful. The entry to her cubicle looked similar to the airlock on the GHO command vehicle. Someone in a suit bulkier than a standard EV suit approached; she assumed he was a doctor or medic by the red cross armband around his left arm.

On the other side, two soldiers were standing guard.

"What the hell are you doing to me?" Rhyll complained, but her throat was dry and her tongue refused to cooperate.

The attendant ignored her guttural mumbling. He tested her straps first, then the tubing, before flicking a small torch in her eyes to examining her pupils. In less than four minutes he turned to leave the room without uttering a word.

"That suit won't save you. You know you're a dead man?" She hated the violence, but knew from experience the death wave would have commenced. Rhyll was more furious at being treated like a lab rat, her human rights totally disregarded. She began struggling with her straps, twisting and alternately pulling and pushing to get free, wary of the cannulas in her arms. Her wrists quickly became raw.

After healing them and resting, she tried again, deciding after the third attempt this method was going to take a long time. This wasn't the doing of Stradjek, he was more concerned with credits and getting her to remove competition. *Who else is after me?*

Rhyll wracked her memory for known enemies. Only DIC and ICON came to mind. GHO seemed more or less on her side, and while she might now be famous, anyone with sufficient means could have grabbed her. The list of resources needed crossed her mind: tracking her or the hoverpod, then hacking into the high-level AI, the fancy EV suits, monitoring and medical equipment, soldiers and a lab.

She removed DIC from her list, assuming they were small fry

with resources limited to the UK. ICON, however, had international connections, were regarded highly by many government — or corporate — organisations, and they had access to high-level AI hoverpods. Those uniforms did remind her of the ICON squad in São Lucas.

This is going to be difficult. The few people she knew expected her to be at Giza. No one was coming to get her, wherever she was.

I have to escape! She relaxed and concentrated on devising a plan. Once everyone died horribly, she'd be stuck here. Whatever was pumping through the tubes — probably saline and perhaps nutrients — would eventually run out, then she'd slowly die. *Or would she?*

"Think! What can I do other than create a death wave and heal?" she muttered.

She had the power of Gaia, according to the shaman ... *So what can Mother Nature do?* "Everything, given time." *Time you and the population haven't got.*

Rhyll recalled manipulating the vines in Manaus. "No plants here." Most of the room was out of her limited view, but she doubted there'd be pot plants in a lab like this.

When the death wave was manifesting, there was thunder and lightning ... static ... and the lights flickered. These thoughts still dwelled in her mind when the door swished open again.

Another bulky EV suit came through. This one had a red stripe around the torso. The individual inside looked shorter than the previous attendant.

"Who are you and what are you doing to me?" she grunted, her voice getting better.

"Miss Ellis. An honour to meet with you at last. I am Professor Miller."

"Where am I?" she rasped, noting his American accent.

The professor readjusted a tube that was out of Rhyll's line of sight. It was a straw for water. She sipped thankfully.

"You're in one of our newer facilities," he said. "We nicknamed it Area 53. Like the renowned Area 51, we do research ... unofficially, and we're delving into your unique abilities."

"I've never heard of it. What happened to Area 51 and 52?" That confirmed to her mind she was somewhere in the USA. *Was it the Democratic Allied States, the Central Commonwealth States, or the Western Union Dan mentioned?*

"Area 51 was always far too popular, especially after the government disclosed UFOs were real a few decades ago. We don't know what happened to 52, but there's a gaping hole where it used to be."

"You're wasting your time. There's no cure to this death wave, you must adapt—"

"Yes. We've seen the newscast. Impressive. But no. We aren't after a cure as such. Our research is more aimed at prevention. We are trying to find out what makes *you* tick. Perhaps then we can replicate it."

"What are you bastards doing to me? Why is my whole body aching?"

"Partly due to the oxygen deprivation we used to keep you unconscious during your flight. We've also taken DNA samples, of course, but I suspect the majority of your pain would be from the bone samples we took. Your blood is also very interesting, extremely rare, though not unique. You've had a total body scan; that was very intriguing also."

"In what way?" She may as well ply him with questions, since he seemed chatty.

"There is a crystal matrix running through your bones — perhaps this is how your blood was transmuted from A-pos to Rh-null? Your mass has increased since your earlier records. We weighed you at 98.62 kilograms because of your very dense bone structure."

"That's' almost double my weight! I suppose that's your clinical way of telling a girl she's fat?"

"On the contrary, it's fascinating. According to your medical records, you weren't born this way. Can you shed any light on this transformation?"

"None that you'd believe. When will you be finished treating me like a specimen? I have things to do, places to go."

"Ah, yes. This quest of yours to *save the world*. Catastrophic as it is, I'm certain technology will prevail over mythology."

"Other scientists thought that too. They're all dead. Your EV suits will be no protection."

"These are not EV suits, they're EMF suits."

"EMF suits?"

"They generate a localised EMF field. The entire facility has a similar setup, nullifying the frequencies of this so-called death wave. This wave somehow affects everyone's immune system — destroys it, while simultaneously intensifying the effects of the many and varied germs and disease we all carry within our bodies. Ingenious."

"Not everyone's immune system is affected," Rhyll muttered.

The professor continued, "The wave is a form of electromagnetism somehow emanating from the ground. Humans have a myriad of germs and microbes running through the system constantly, but our antibodies are sufficient to deal with them. Did you know the bubonic plague is still out there, as is AIDS, SARS and all its variants, as well as TB? With today's vaccines and medical treatment, these are treatable, and only rarely fatal."

That's what's missing, and why I feel off, I've been disconnected from the earth. "Can your science explain how this wave occurs? Why it's spreading, and why in those specific locations?"

"Not yet, but we'll get there, given time and sufficient resources."

"Not that you have all that much time. Who do you work for?"

"We have many avenues of support. You've been here for over twelve hours. We obviously need continuous access to samples to study and analyse. You're extremely valuable, your other traits are a bonus."

"Milking my *rare* blood all that time I imagine? I don't

suppose you've considered my human rights, or the ethics of keeping a person incarcerated against their will?"

"Oh, we aren't barbarians. We do have an ethics committee, of course — we meet weekly — but considering the potential saving of human lives, the needs of the many outweigh yours. Harsh but pragmatic."

"Any chance of being released to a cell? Maybe treated like a human?"

He shrugged inside his suit. "That's out of my hands. It's a security matter."

She had an idea. And hated it, but as he said, the needs of the many ... "Enjoy the rest of your short life."

The professor's departing comment was muffled in his suit. After exiting the airlock, he went to check the monitor stations, where everyone deferred to him.

The pain was still there. She concentrated on a bit of healing, rendering it to a dull ache. A light panel dimmed slightly. Her thoughts went back to devising a method of escape.

The powers of Mother Earth ... Again, given time, nature could do amazing things; erosion forming wonders like the Grand Canyon, volcanoes, cyclones, thunder and lightning ...

She was isolated from the ground. *Or am I?* "You have veins of crystallisation running through your bones," the professor had said. *Can that be a clue? Am I able to do these things? Am I not Nature incarnate?*

Light panels ran on electricity ... *Can I use that? Electricity?*

Once again, she relaxed her mind and focused on her surroundings. She used to do this all those times when in the jungles — sensing what was around her — like she'd sensed Cataleya, Benigno and Felipe sneaking up on her in Manaus.

After what seemed hours, she dozed.

Nothing had changed when she woke up; people were still manning their desks in the dim room. She sipped from her straw and continued her detecting. Before she dozed, she was feeling where the electric currents were running behind the panels. With her eyes closed it looked like thin, faint lines of light in the darkness. *Like the streaks of light at night from cars in time lapse photos.*

Rhyll's next step was to try to manipulate it. She had no conscious idea how to do it, but she had no idea how to do most of what she had done before.

How did I get the vines to grow? How did I heal?

The simplest idea to her was to visualise it; encouraging the lines of light to merge as she had with Ileana's fractured elbow.

She tried to blank her mind from other thoughts, and concentrated on her surroundings. The walls, floor and ceiling appeared to her as a solid mass, but as she expanded her senses the structure gradually became a bland, grey haze.

Her head throbbed, but she did manage to see indistinct lines of energy running through the haze. Before she dropped off into exhaustion, she opened her eyes. One of the panels flickered and darkened.

People came and went, replacing her catheter bag, giving her a sponge bath, and repairing the panel. From that she learnt the green armband signified maintenance. All the visors of their EMF suits were mirrored, so she had no idea who was who, male or female. No one spoke to her, but one person did provide a sweet-flavoured drink when replacing her water. When she thanked them, they merely nodded.

Left alone, Rhyll continued with her experimentation, extending her sensing range outside her room, even as far as the monitors and beyond, though there was some resistance. She also noted the security cameras scattered around the rooms, including hers. *They're going next.*

She was getting better at making the light panel black out. Better and faster. Previously, it had barely fizzled; this time it flashed and sparked before darkening. Rhyll tried the same thing with the camera.

The sensitive smoke detectors lit up and made a soft but piercing wail. To her reckoning, it was less than a minute before a soldier moved in with an extinguisher. A technician came to investigate the panel soon after the soldier left, but this time he isolated the circuit instead of repairing it, and he replaced the camera. Whether it was useful or not, it confirmed the green armband was for maintenance personnel.

Rhyll looked for the change caused by the isolated circuit, realising it didn't matter now that she could create a surge to jump the wires; when she did so, in her mind she saw the arc of current. It reminded her of a vid she'd seen of a Van de Graf generator.

She was getting the knack of it, but the next time she would have to do something drastic before they became suspicious of her. For that, more rest was required.

Refreshed after her snooze, Rhyll repeatedly clenched and relaxed her fists, doing the same for her legs; it was the only form of exercise she could do here, and it helped increase her blood circulation, if only slightly.

With no idea how those responsible for her incarceration would react, she drank as much of her nutrient drink as she could stomach before conducting a final test. Her improved sensing registered much more of the complex, and she noticed bright areas where there was a merging of powerful electrical conduits.

Fuse boxes?

There was much more power in those areas, and more power meant bigger zaps. Rhyll relaxed and concentrated on the nearest one. The electricity was most vulnerable ... *there!*

The arcing current, much more potent than what she could achieve with the light circuits, fried the fuse box. In her mind, there was a massive flash before many paths of converging currents vanished instantly, leaving the faintest trail which was separate to the fuse box. With the bulk of the nearby energy removed, she could now discern power much further afield. She felt the resistance disappear.

Rhyll opened her eyes. The area was now darker, lit only by dull orange emergency lighting. Through the windows she could see silhouettes moving quickly in confusion in the adjacent room. Below her, the mechanical sound had stopped. Her surrounds felt different. *No EMF?* There was a very faint connection with the land now and ... *it was a couple of hours after sunset.*

It took at least five minutes passed before soldiers arrived. Powered by the emergency generator, the airlock provided entry as they cycled through in pairs. Each soldier had bright lights on a headband, keeping their hands free.

Rhyll noticed they had swapped their guns for tasers. The intense glow she could see with her enhanced senses sparked an idea.

"What's happening out there?" she asked, squinting in the harsh glare of their lights.

"You're being moved. You gonna behave, or do we drug you?"

She doubted she could escape four armed soldiers, but just to move freely would be wonderful. "I'll try to behave."

They quickly ushered in a female medic who efficiently removed the cannulas and placed bandages to stop the bleeding. She then pointed and spoke sternly to the soldiers who grudgingly stepped back to the side wall.

They continued to watch Rhyll warily, tasers at the ready.

"I have to remove the catheter. It will feel uncomfortable," the medic advised Rhyll.

Rhyll nodded. *Finally, some decency!* She realised the soldiers had been moved for her privacy.

"Thank you for *that*," she said softly to the medic. There was no indication of her rank or name anywhere on her suit, just the red-crossed armband.

"It's fine." The medic carefully lifted Rhyll's gown.

The catheter removal while conscious did feel extremely uncomfortable.

"All done." She lowered the gown.

The medic collected her equipment and a soldier quickly ushered her out, while another undid Rhyll's straps.

Once she was released they had to help her climb off the bed, since she had been immobile for several days.

"What about my shoes?"

"You won't be needing them," a soldier replied smugly.

Two men cycled through first, then she was helped through by the third; the fourth came through last, and they slowly made their way down a long corridor.

"Looks like a big power outage," she noted, fishing for information.

"Yep. Main junction box took out this section—"

"Shut it, corporal," the one in charge ordered.

The orange lights went on for quite a while. The corridor ended at a large, robust metal door.

"Does that mean no EMF protection?" She knew the answer anyway.

"We can still drug you," the gruff soldier said. "Best to keep your mouth shut." Now facing the large door, he punched in a security code.

This door was on a different circuit. As the door opened with a hiss of positive pressure, two EMF-suited individuals armed with tasers appeared on the other side.

"We'll take her from here," the taller one said.

Rhyll briefly closed her eyes and concentrated. The suits had a faint halo effect — she hadn't noticed that with the previous EMF suit. The large door swung closed.

Is that what EMF looks like? she wondered. It was a simple matter now to discern the currents coursing through the suits. As she was dragged away, Rhyll considered this new development, deducing that she could now see a larger range of the spectrum.

Rhyll could feel her feet now and use her legs more confidently, but allowed the guards to think she was still docile. She also noticed a more military aspect to this section by the signage and the drab paint — reminding her of some of the barracks she'd seen.

"What's the next plan? More testing for this guinea pig by Professor Miller?"

They paused at another security door.

"We're just escorting you to a safe place. You'll be seen to shortly."

No other personnel had made an appearance, and she wondered how long that would last.

"May I sit? I feel ill."

After a brief hesitation, one nodded, and they lowered her to the floor by the wall. "Five minutes," one said.

"Thank you."

She could see their lips moving through the visors as they used an internal commlink to talk without her hearing. Rhyll closed her eyes, letting them think she was calming her nausea, and concentrated. She examined the area around her, both physically and mentally. Their halos were bright, but not as bright as the charges in their tasers. Other than the cables for the lighting and power points, she noted the position and number of security cameras.

Her strategy, as with the energy lines at the junction box, was to visualise the electricity overloading. The cameras were easy enough to short out. Since the distance between the suits was a lot bigger than the distance between the wires at the junction box, though, this would take far more concentration.

Fortunately, the right moment came when they turned to collect her. Their electro-magnetic fields merged. She forced the arcing. In her mind, like the Van de Graph, the discharge of the suits flared but it combined with the powerpacks of both tasers. Intense, jagged spiderwebs of current flared more powerful than she'd expected — or wanted.

The suit halos immediately vanished. Both guards spasmed and dropped to the floor, twitching as smoke issued from several scorched rends where the power surge had been the most concentrated.

Rhyll didn't think she'd forget the horrid looks on their faces as the pain hit them.

Even though the population of the world was at stake, she deeply regretted the deaths of these men, promising to herself to be more careful when using these powers.

CHAPTER TWENTY

A<small>LL WAS SILENT</small>. N<small>O ALARMS WERE RAISED THAT SHE COULD HEAR</small>.
Rhyll used the wall as support while she moved ahead. Maps were displayed at the many intersections. Her increased sensory range gave her a reasonable idea of the layout of the complex, but the signage now gave those areas names. There were four floors above her and two below. Each time She shorted the cameras, knowing that it would garner curiosity. She hoped the frequent power fluctuations might not make them too suspicious of her activities.

"That's something I'll deal with as it comes," she muttered as she continued in search of the hijacked hoverpod. Considering where she was and some of the tech she'd seen, it was evident they had the capabilities of hacking into the sophisticated AI. The reference to Area 53 made her consider top secret projects and alien aircraft like those supposed to be in Area 51.

Her heightened senses alerted her of movement ahead. On her left was a sealed door to a vacant room. Rhyll touched the pad next to it, creating a small surge of energy. The seal popped and she stepped in, quickly pushing it closed behind her.

Rhyll stood by the door as she listened for the person to pass by. Instead, the door opened and a female figure stepped inside. Rhyll swiftly caused the suit's powerpack to short-circuit. It wasn't as violent as the tasers going off, so this woman still lived.

Think, girl! You can't go zapping everyone.

She sent her mind out to see where she needed to go and how many people were down here. This floor had a few personnel but there were many more on the other levels. It wouldn't be long until the two dead soldiers were missed; she'd better hurry up. When she found the camera, she didn't short it, but followed the power to another junction box. She shorted that instead, taking out the cameras in this whole section. *I should have done that earlier.*

Further along the corridor she sensed a lab similar to the one she had just left, and beyond the monitoring room was a lift. If she was correct, there was an area large enough to be a hangar on the top floor, which was still thirty metres below ground. Hopefully her pod was there. Although it was compromised, she needed to locate her gear and it was the best place to start.

Rhyll stripped the woman of her EMF suit, noting the purple armband. It was heavy and slow going and putting it on wasn't much easier. She stopped several times when hearing people walk by. The garb was too large on her, and bumbling around in an oversized EMF suit would mark her as an outsider as much as traipsing around in a short hospital gown would.

She swore at the wasted time and climbed out, discarding the idea. More people were passing at a faster pace and she sensed a few were now gathered around the two guards back down the corridor.

I reckon they're definitely looking for me now, she thought.

Stepping out into the now empty corridor she strode quickly towards the elevator, her bare feet making little sound. She had to increase her pace when she sensed two more EMF suits descending. If they were passing, great, but it could be awkward if they stopped on her floor.

The chime pinged.

"Shit." The doors slid open. She was still halfway across the monitor room, and before she could dive under the long bench with the monitors, the two figures went straight to the airlock and cycled through into the lab. There was a single bed similar to the one she had just vacated, tubes and all.

Nice to know those visors have limited vision.

Rhyll quickly crawled to the elevator as the doors were closing, putting her arm in front of the sensors. The doors opened again and she scuttled in. If they noticed her or the doors, she had no idea. They didn't shout any warning that she heard.

Internal comms, stupid. Rhyll chastised herself and hit the button for the top floor, and waited as the lift sped upwards. She identified one figure standing near the lift doors on the hangar level.

Now knowing what to do, when the elevator doors opened she reached out and shorted the suit's powerpack like before. He had no taser, only a pistol. Once the guard slumped, she dragged him into the lift. She briefly contemplated taking the weapon, then shook her head.

There were five figures waiting by the lift on the various levels below.

So nobody else could use the elevator and surprise her by emerging unexpectedly on her floor, she reached for the buttons and caused a power surge. There was a crackling sound and smoke issued from the panel.

"That'll give me a few minutes, until they decide to use the stairs," she told herself. She stepped out into the empty corridor that stretched left and right. The lift doors remained open behind her.

The sensitive smoke detectors started a loud intermittent buzzing.

"Shit!" Rhyll quickened her pace to the hangar and warily stepped inside. Despite the urgency, she stopped in awe.

As expected, the hoverpod was there, along with other pods, but further back in the shadows was an alien spaceship that dwarfed everything around it. She stifled a laugh, thinking of those blurry pictures of UFOs she'd seen, ovular discs looking like kids' toys. This was a flattened disc, quickly thickening towards the centre, forming a dome top and bottom. There was an odd sensation to un-see it, as if it wasn't really there—

Rhyll shook her head. She couldn't afford to be distracted by this, no matter how astonishing it was, and she ran to her pod. Thurston's drone lay discarded on the hangar floor.

As expected, they'd trashed her pack, and her clothes were strewn across the floor and chairs. Grabbing her clothes, she quickly ripped off the gown and dressed.

But how thoroughly did they really search? she wondered.

Rhyll sat on the floor and slid on her back under the console. It looked the same as the last time she saw it. She pushed at the panel to widen the split, and reached in to where she hoped the artefacts, tablet and notebook remained hidden.

Yes!

She withdrew the items and after a quick kiss of each, popped them into her pack with everything else. *Damn, they took my phones!*

The echo of many boots coming down the corridor reached her ears. Hiding inside the pod was pointless. Taking her pack, she darted out and used the bulk of the pod while moving further from the door, passing the UFO.

Rhyll raced around to the far side of the weird craft as the hangar door burst wide open. When she crouched, she saw beams of light sweeping across the expansive floor and stabbing into the darker recesses of the large hangar as five soldiers rushed in.

The UFO had no landing gear to block them from her view — or, conversely, to hide *her* from *them*.

The craft is floating.

"Shit! They'll see my legs!" This was a new dilemma.

There was nothing else around her to use for cover; the distance to the other pods was too great. Now much closer, she understood why the UFO looked so dark. It absorbed light! *Maybe enough to hide me?*

With seconds to spare, she took a few steps back, then ran and jumped onto the hull of the alien ship. Surprisingly, momentum caused her to slide much further than anticipated. The surface felt slimy. It was tricky climbing, and there were no seams or panels to grip. She gave up and lay motionless, but even so, felt like she was sliding off.

As if it's almost frictionless!

The torchlight swept the floor and under the craft as the soldiers spread out; one returned to the door; another entered the pod and the others spread out to cover more of the hanger. The one in the pod quickly came out, waving her medical robe.

Abruptly, the other soldiers turned, ran to the door and left the hangar. She waited, following their faint energy signatures as they checked the other rooms along the corridor.

It only lasted a couple of seconds, but sliding over the hull was the most fun she'd had for a long time. Rhyll dropped lightly to the floor in bare feet. With no further distractions, she focused on locating her diamond.

Gradually she could make out the slight nuances of the electrical fields and the life energy of people. And, not knowing how she did it — like not knowing how she accomplished many things — Rhyll gradually filtered out the white noise and studied what was left. The remaining brightness was one floor down and the other side of this underground bunker.

Found you.

Weariness hit her like a truck. She reflexively reached out for balance but her hands slid off the spacecraft's surface. Rhyll tumbled to the hard floor. Catching her breath, she staggered to the pod, climbed inside, got the door closed and slumped into the seat.

By her internal clock, she'd been unconscious for an hour. Her water flask still sat in the seat pocket, along with a bag of stale chips. She contemplated her predicament as she consumed the lot, washing the chips down with the bland water.

"Computer, activate ... Power on." The control panel remained dark. After flicking switches randomly, she guessed the pod had been drained of power.

"Not that I know how to fly the damn thing." What could she do now? Her eyes scanned the interior for some alternative, and her mind, checking down an imaginary list of options, none of them feasible, happened on—

The drone! Looking out the window, she sighed in relief to see nobody had returned to the hangar after their initial search. She climbed out, jumping the couple of steps to the floor.

The drone's powerpack had been pulled. "Clearly, which is why I didn't sense it before." She sat on the steps. "First job, retrieve the diamond ... but how?"

As she extended her mind, she noticed the surface was ten metres above the hangar roof, five of which was reinforced concrete, including a thick metal mesh. The concept of a Faraday cage came to mind.

Was that for the EMF shield Miller mentioned?

The floor below had many active people moving from area to area, floor to floor. Her refined senses filtered what she now perceived as a power supply, and she spent a bit of time examining the points the energy was flowing to: computers, monitors, lighting and other sundry equipment.

"Laboratories, I'm guessing." And her diamond was in the thick of it. There were guards stationed at the lab doors. A plan was needed to get past not only the guards but also the scientists.

Pushing her mind further afield resulted in a raging headache and several ideas.

Each wing had its own power source and EMF mesh, but the previous wing was now almost deserted and the EMF shield was deactivated. She could do the same thing here, couldn't she? Taking out the EMF for the entire complex would expose them all to the death wave.

Rhyll wondered how much exposure was a death sentence.

Was there even a death wave here? She couldn't sense it, but that was possibly the effect of the shielding. This led her to wondering again: *Where am I?*

Rhyll decided she needed more information before she acted. No point wasting time and energy on a plan doomed to fail before it was initiated. If she got outside, she knew she could work out where she was more precisely.

She went to the far wall of the hangar, where there was bound to be some emergency exit or maintenance access. Sure enough, in the far corner she found rungs in the wall, rising to a hatch in the ceiling. The ladder was hidden in shadow.

Climbing to the top, she found an electronic panel similar to those on other doors she'd seen, and quickly shorted it. The hatch was heavy. She climbed a couple more rungs, put her shoulder to it and pushed with her legs, straining at the effort. Once past the halfway point, it swung open.

She was greeted by a ten-metre shaft devoid of any security. If she took too long they'd either catch her in the shaft or apprehend her when she emerged. With that as an incentive, and utilising the energy of a teenager in flight, Rhyll raced as quickly as she could, her foot slipping only once before she reached the next heavy hatch. It was the same as before and within a minute after shorting the panel she was outside, breathing the cold night air and rubbing her strained shoulder from forcing the hatches.

The whirring sound of hoverpods was getting louder. The opening was in a clearing, and it was a mad dash for cover — and even that was only stunted shrubs, mostly juniper. She had to be careful: there was a lot of prickly pear and agave. She had no allergy concerns, but they still stung.

There was a clear sky, but the moon was nowhere to be seen on this wintry evening. Taking in her surroundings at a glance, she saw that, going by the myriad of lights behind her to the west and north, she was high on a plateau overlooking a large town. The horizon looked rugged, indicating mountains and large rocky outcroppings.

Another aircraft could be heard, getting much louder. She saw the landing lights. She was next to an airfield? Keeping low and dodging through the undergrowth, she headed in the direction where she'd seen the nearest streetlights.

The exit hatch she'd used was now a couple of hundred metres behind her; a row of buildings and the airfield control tower stood in front. Looking back, she saw that a drone was now hovering over the open hatch, flooding the area with light, while another scoured the terrain around it.

Other sounds, rising to impinge on her ears, announced the rapid approach of several ground vehicles.

"Time to move, girl." She kept low and dodged from tree to tree as she got closer to the buildings. Veering away from vehicle lights, she noticed the car park. It was brightly lit, so she remained in the shadows of the scrub and skirted around the perimeter.

"What the hell are you doing?" she asked herself as she rested against the rough bark of a tree trunk. "All you had to do was find out where you were!"

Her feet were starting to hurt. It had been too long since she'd been running barefoot in the jungles, and her soles had softened. She took a moment to heal them.

The headlights of a car flashed past as it left the parking lot. Luckily she was in the shadow of the tree. Under the awning of the building she saw a sign: *Sedona Airport*.

"Sedona?" The name was vaguely familiar. The aircraft landed with the sound of skidding tyres. *Area 53 is under an airport?*

The immediate area around her was devoid of people. The pods had moved further away, as had the vehicles but they'd swing back soon enough. Rhyll sat down, caught her breath and relaxed, letting her mind absorb her surroundings and whereabouts. Now that she was free of the EMF shielding, what she learnt surprised even her.

As a kid she could determine weather and directions easily.

What she was feeling now was different, she knew her location with far greater accuracy; smack in the middle of Arizona.

"And I'm a hell of a long way from Giza!"

Now she knew where she was, and there was no death wave here. The closest one was spreading from Mount Shasta in northern California, roughly a thousand miles northwest of here. Rhyll wondered why that was the case. She had certainly been aggravated enough.

"Perhaps the EMF shield *did* work?"

"This is all nice but with no one knowing where I am, no money and no way of communicating ... I need a distraction so I can retrieve the diamond. That's *all* you need to do for now!"

Her keener senses detected a huge energy source. *The substation for the airport?* Rhyll smiled. It tied in with the underground facility. *That's handy.*

With her new-found expertise and so much energy, forcing the arc was easier. The ensuing explosion echoed across the valley, sending sparks high and starting small fires. As expected, the entire area blacked out and emergency lighting kicked in.

Rhyll heard sirens minutes later, but her attention returned to the approaching pods and ATVs. She dived to the sandy ground and crawled, using the low scrub to hide. Once the pods and vehicles moved away, she ran back to the hatch. Part of her mind said she was crazy to do this, the other part said they'd never expect her to use her escape route as a method to return.

"And, they probably don't think I'd risk going back for the diamond."

Upon reaching the hatch, she climbed down carefully and quietly in case they'd put a guard below. They did, but just the one. *They're not completely stupid.*

Rhyll spied him standing near the base of the ladder in an EMF suit not paying any attention. *I wonder if he can hear me?*

She felt in her pockets for the grit that had accumulated during her crawling. Sure enough, she found the pebble that had rubbed against her thigh. She lobbed it at the UFO. It hit and slid along the hull. The near frictionless surface hardly made a sound. She cursed herself for her idiocy, but when the rock fell to the hard floor, it echoed loud and clear in the empty silent hangar.

The guard didn't flinch. She'd assumed right: he couldn't hear anything. "No doubt relying on his internal comms," she mused as she climbed down.

Once again ensuring not to overdo it, she shorted the guard's suit, but wasn't in a position to catch him as he fell heavily to the floor. With an effort, she dragged him to the pod and pushed him underneath, then entered the pod, refilled her flask and took a drink before setting off to the stairs. She paused by the door and checked beyond.

Her senses picked up only two individuals in the labs below. *Guards?* There was a mass of life energy heading up one of the stairways. *Evacuating the scientists.*

She jogged to another set of stairs further along the corridor, one that wasn't being used. As expected, the entire area was illuminated with emergency lighting only.

The floor below was no different, and the dull orange lighting created many shadowy areas to conceal oneself in. Rhyll paused regularly to check on energy signatures of any patrolling guards, and for her diamond.

The guards were stationary, but positioned near the lab where her target was. She was certain not everyone had their external microphones muted, and she'd use that to her benefit if need be. Another obvious consideration was that someone would come looking here eventually. She hoped she'd not be here by then.

The walls of the passage only rose halfway; the top half were glass panels to the ceiling. This gave her the opportunity to see in, but also meant anybody on the other side would be able to see her. Peering through the glass, she saw a patchwork of cubicles, all connected by similar passages. Some cubicles were large, some small, each with its own array of strange and varied testing equipment. She did recognise a spectrometer, much like the one at the Manaus University, but that was it.

She crawled the majority of the way to the laboratory she wanted. The guards hadn't moved, but they were facing each other in conversation. She could barely hear them, and every now and then an arm would wave as if explaining a point. So far all the soldiers she had encountered here were males. A cursory sensing indicated their EMF suit halo. *And they had tasers.*

She needed something to distract them; to get their halos to merge. Other than grit and dust, there was nothing useful in her pockets. The hallway was empty, and she didn't have time to go hunting for anything. She chuckled as a ridiculous idea came to mind; one she indirectly attributed to Dan and his prudishness.

I wonder if other men feel the same way?

Rhyll took her top off, stood up and walked boldly towards them. Forgetting the limited vision of their visors, she was within arm's reach before they noticed her presence. By then, she simply reached out and caused their suits to overload.

Both guards fell against each other as they collapsed.

This is getting too easy! Rhyll pulled her shirt back on. Something tangled in her hair briefly. A quick tug was all she needed to free it. The forgotten ankh fell to the floor. As she bent down to pick it up, a hand gripped her ankle.

The suit enhanced their strength and it felt like her ankle was being crushed. Before she reacted, the guard tasered her. Or tried. The moment the needles hit her thigh, the taser overloaded and exploded, blowing the man's hand off. He screamed before losing consciousness.

Shocked at the outcome, Rhyll pocketed the ankh and used his swipe card. Her hand was shaking and it took several attempts before she opened the door. With her thigh now numb she stumbled into the lab.

There were dozens of drawers and secured lockers, large and small. She paused. Her diamond was … *there.* As expected, the drawer was locked.

They may have evacuated, but they're not sloppy enough to leave their artefacts lying about. A quick look around gave no clue how to open the solid metal drawers. *What, no key left on a keyboard?*

She hadn't come all this way to fail. If she didn't get the diamond now, there was no way they'd let her try again once they realised how keen she was to retrieve it. Her senses picked up life forces coming down the stairs. *Is it a normal patrol,* she wondered, *or did they hear something from the guard's comms?*

Dragging her leg, Rhyll returned to the guards. Even as she did so, she thought how pointless it was. *No way would they have authorisation to get into these things.*

The lockers, being metallic, gave her an idea. *Could a charge from the taser do enough damage?* She heaved the guard over and grabbed the one remaining taser. *Or would the charge fry the locker contents?*

"That gun, on the other hand ..." She dropped the taser into another pocket and reached for the gun. Dashing back in, she aimed the muzzle at the lock.

Click.

"Damn safety!" She flicked it, aimed and fired. There was some damage, but not enough. She fired again at a different angle and checked. *Bingo!* When she tried to pull, the drawer opened partially. She put the gun on top and wiggled the drawer with increasing force until it opened, but it slid only a few inches before jamming.

"Fuck it!" She shoved the drawer in frustration. The whole unit flew back, hit the far wall and bounced forwards before toppling onto its side. Glass from the shattered window rained down, sending shards everywhere. In surprise and shock at her strength, Rhyll stepped forward, unconcerned about the glass.

The drawer was still partially open, but now buckled. She carefully swept most of the glass away and knelt, blindly reaching in to feel for her diamond. She touched something cool, but as it wasn't the diamond; she ignored it, reaching deeper, spurred by the sound of a door further down the corridor opening.

Idiot. I bet they heard the shots! See what panic does! Rhyll took a calming breath. *Use your senses!* she berated herself again. Trying to remove her arm, she found it was stuck! Something cold and clammy wrapped around her searching fingers.

"What the fuck is that!" *Calm the farm*, she chided herself. Gently, she twisted her arm here, slid it there, and it came free with barely a bruise or scratch.

There was something black wrapped around her right hand, reaching halfway up her forearm, looking like one of those old-fashioned gloves she'd seen in movies. She flicked her hand, but whatever it was refused to budge. As she knelt trying to pull it off, her eyes focused on her blue diamond among the shards of broken glass.

"I'll take that, thank you," she said.

The moment her left hand grasped the diamond, she felt calmer. Breathing a sigh of relief, Rhyll pocketed the diamond, then crawled behind the fallen locker and concentrated. The *glove* would have to wait, as she sensed five life-forces rapidly making their way towards the lab. Behind her was the now windowless opening to an adjoining cubicle which led to another passage.

As she crawled to the wall, she spied the gun. Glad she had so many pockets, she slipped the gun into one. *That's why I love cargo pants!* She slithered over the window ledge, hissing when she felt an edge cut her hip and thigh.

With no time to spare, she continued crawling to the far door and along the passage towards the stairs she used. After five cubicles she guessed there was enough distance that she would be obscured by the dim emergency lighting and several walls of glass. She covered the remaining distance in a crouching run, staying below the window level.

At the door to the stairway she paused. The guards had spread out to search the nearest cubicles. It would only be another minute before they saw her trail of blood. She glanced down at her thigh. The trousers were torn and bloodied. *And only three days old.* She slipped into the stairway and bolted back to the hangar, determined not to panic again.

Back in the pod, she sat and drank some more water, then

healed herself enough to stop the bleeding. The torn trousers would have to wait. She grabbed the console to swivel in the chair to check the hangar was clear.

There was a sharp tingle from the glove as the console flashed.

What was that? Stupidly, her mind thought of those wet paint signs, *Do not touch.* She touched the panel again, but this time hung on. The console came to life and the tingle prevailed, though to a lesser degree.

"I thought you were flat," she said to the pod, thinking the AI would respond.

"It was."

Not the AI ... Sensing the strange thought in her mind she looked at the glove warily. *Who?*

"More of a what, not who. I am a construct, not an entity."

As she sat there perplexed, soldiers burst into the hangar. Rhyll swore.

"You are concerned?"

"Good guess."

"Not a guess. Mere deduction of the evidence: your evasiveness, your rising heart rate and breathing."

She looked around, thinking at least she should close the door and make it harder for them to get her.

"I require you to touch the surface."

Rhyll hesitated, then placed her hand on the console. "Why?"

The door swung close and sealed. A moment later the sound of someone pounding on the hull reached her.

"Shit!" *The suit's enhanced strength would damage the hull.*

As the pounding increased there was a zap and a flash outside. Rhyll saw two guards fly backwards. They landed badly on the hangar floor, unmoving.

"What did you do?" she asked the glove, thinking how ludicrous it would look. It gave *talk to the hand* a whole new meaning.

"I perceived a potential hull breach and defended this craft."

"How?"

"A quick modification to charge the door. The metallic structure is a poor conductor, so the defence was minimal, but the shielding of their suits increased the effect. However, repeated discharges will drain the residual power supply."

"You modified the hull?"

"No. Only a minor change in the circuits pertaining to the door."

"Can you fly?"

"No."

"Bugger."

"It was not the intention of my designer."

"Okay. I get it." Rhyll pulled the gun from her pocket as she saw the guards all aiming their weapons at the pod. "I don't suppose you can make the hull bulletproof?"

"Not in the time frame required as I have not attained full functionality. I can make this craft fly. Is that what you meant earlier?"

"Yes! Can you fly this pod?" Rhyll articulated the question.

"As long as I remain in contact."

Transferring the gun to her left hand, she touched the console. The engine rumbled to life and the pod lifted swiftly to the roof.

"Shall I open the exit doors?"

"Good idea."

A large door in the hangar ceiling slowly slid open. Above it, there was another large door; this too slid open revealing the clear night sky. Leaf matter and dust rained down.

"A better idea would have been to utilise the other craft."

"What other craft? The UFO?"

"I sense we are in agreement."

Bullets peppered the pod's hull as it rose into the sky. Below, the city night lights were now visible. The console beeped loudly as another aircraft veered away erratically.

"Shit!" Rhyll instinctively ducked, but maintained contact with the console as the underside of an aeroplane shot past. She sat upright, feeling foolish. The alarm stopped as quickly as it had started.

"There are no further imminent collisions."

"Go back to what you said about the UFO. I didn't know we could get into it. Is that where you belong?" she asked.

"No, but it is a far more advanced vehicle." The voice continued without inflection or acknowledgement of the near fatal crash.

"H... How do we get into it?" Rhyll took a deep breath. *I'm going in a UFO!*

There was a pause.

"How—" Before Rhyll repeated the question, the voice was back in her head.

"Modification of this pod's primitive circuitry was necessary. I have just communicated with the alien craft. You are now able to enter."

"Is it safe?" she asked, as the pod quickly returned to the hangar. Far faster than she could imagine, the pod manoeuvred behind the larger ship as more bullets pinged on the fuselage.

"Irrelevant. This pod is about to lose power; a power cell has been compromised."

A part of the dark hull of the looming UFO distorted, revealing and even darker interior.

"Your entrance."

The hoverpod glided closer as its door swung up directly opposite the new entrance.

Bewildered at the speed at which things were happening, Rhyll was halfway to the door before she remembered her pack. She grabbed it and shoved the gun inside it. At the threshold she jumped to the other ship, fully expecting to slide off the slick surface, but as she stepped onto the exterior, she found her feet had traction this time.

As soon as she left, the hoverpod swiftly rose and flew around the hangar, scattering the soldiers. The pod crashed into the wall by the door, blocking the entrance. There was no explosion but everyone managed to avoid it; some lay on the floor groaning, others were silent and motionless.

"They are merely unconscious. I do not take life."

Somewhat relieved, Rhyll paused before she stepped warily inside thinking the glove hadn't really answered her last question.

Is it safe?

THE END

Continued in Book 3

ACKNOWLEDGMENTS

I'd like to send a huge thank you to both:

Belinda Crawford who created the covers; https://designedbyboots.com

Noel Osualdini for his excellent editorial assistance.

My original beta-reader crew: Peter J Aldin, Stephen Kerwin, Aaron Cordy, and a big welcome to Karl Martin, Heather Stone, Doug Switzer and Scott Burnard for all their perseverance and politely pointing out my failings.

And finally but most importantly, my wife Morag for putting up with my absent-minded rantings, and all my friends. I'm slowly learning what that glazed stare means.

ABOUT THE AUTHOR

Andre Jones was born in Wollongong, NSW Australia and currently resides in Melbourne with his very understanding Scottish wife, a British Shorthair cat, and more recently, a Jack Russell Terrier pup.

As a child he devoured the works of Enid Blyton, Tolkien, McCAffrey, Asimov, Heinlein and Bradbury just to name a few. As a young adult, he got lost in the many and varied roleplaying games, including MERP, GURPS, Harn, Skyrealms of Jorune, good old D&D *(and its many variants)* and Traveller … and spent far too much time on video games like Skyrim.

He wore many hats including; Security Officer, Police Officer, Park Ranger and finally as a Petty Officer in the Royal Australian Navy for 18 years *(sadly, his role-playing stopped there for too long)*.

As a Navy Veteran, his retirement has provided the opportunity to write, roleplay, draw and potter to his heart's content.